STEDMAN AND JOANNA—A LOVE IN BONDAGE

Dedicated Love in the Eighteenth Century

Beryl Gilroy

VANTAGE PRESS
New York

To the memory of Pat Gilroy (1919–1975),
remembered with love and gratitude.

FIRST EDITION

All rights reserved, including the right of
reproduction in whole or in part in any form.

Copyright © 1991 by Beryl Gilroy

Published by Vantage Press, Inc.
516 West 34th Street, New York, New York 10001

Manufactured in the United States of America
ISBN: 0-533-09498-4

Library of Congress Catalog Card No.: 90-90501

0 9 8 7 6 5 4 3 2 1

Special thanks to my friends Peter and Emma Roos of Oakland, California, who helped me recover from the exhaustion of writing this demanding book by allowing me to rest undisturbed in their home.

Contents

Foreword

Why was a Scotsman fighting in a Dutch colony on the coast of South America against African slaves? Asking the question that way assumes that the eighteenth century was much like the twentieth; answering it allows us to understand the differences between them.

First of all, it is important to note that nationalism was only beginning at the end of the eighteenth century to become the force that it would later be. John Gabriel Stedman's own life illustrates that change. The male members of his family had been either soldiers or ministers. His own father served in the Scots Brigade, part of the army of the Dutch republic, and married a native of that country. Stedman followed his father into the brigade.

Armies in the eighteenth century consisted of professional soldiers of any nationality: the French Revolution introduced the idea of the nation in arms and brought to an end the era of multinational armies. In Stedman's lifetime the change occurred as a result of the American Revolution, when the Dutch and British found themselves in conflict and the Scots Brigade was disbanded in 1783, being incorporated into the British army in 1794. So for a soldier of one country to fight for another *as a matter of course* was not unusual then. Even if Stedman's mother had not been Dutch, he might have served in the Dutch army or, alternatively in the army of another European power. Stedman's choice of returning to Britain was particularly poignant since in 1782 he had married a Dutch woman.

The second point to make in answering the question is about the importance in the eighteenth century of colonies independent since 1975, like Surinam. The plantation colonies of Britain, France, and the Dutch republic were regarded as worth fighting for. The Dutch had been the pioneers of the conversion of these colonies into profitable possessions. In the seventeenth century they had occupied Brazil and expanded its sugar production. Even before their expulsion by the Portuguese in the midseventeenth century, they had begun to transfer sugar production to their own small colonies and to those of other European powers in the Caribbean region. In Surinam in 1713 there were 171 sugar plantations. Sugar continued to expand until about 1750, when difficulties in securing enough labor forced diversification into crops like cotton, cacao, and coffee, which were less labor-intensive. Trade with the republic increased until 1775: Surinam was to the Dutch what Santo Domingo, now Haiti, was to the French in the late eighteenth century: the centrepiece of their American empire. So in the eighteenth century these small countries were worth fighting for, either against other European powers or against the rebellious labor force.

The mention of the labor force and the comparison with Santo Domingo bring us to the final part of the answer. The sugar, and other, plantations in the Caribbean area had for their labor force enslaved Africans. Attempts to enslave the original American peoples had ended in failure, either because European diseases and overwork had killed them, as on the islands of Cuba, Puerto Rico, and Hispaniola (now Haiti and the Dominican Republic), military expeditions had slaughtered them, as on the smaller islands, or they had retreated from the invading Europeans, as in the mainland colonies. The French and British especially had experimented with white convicts and contracted laborers, but the supply of these could never meet the demand. The midseventeenth century expansion of sugar production led to a growing reliance on enslaved Africans, establishing a common pattern for all the Caribbean territories. By the end of the seventeenth century in Surinam there were about ten Africans to every European; by the end of the eighteenth century the ratio was about eighteen to one. In most other European colonies at that later time the ratios were more like the earlier one. This unusually small proportion of European inhabitants in Surinam may help us to understand the Dutch reputation in the eighteenth century for unusual harshness and cruelty to their slaves. Their methods are best seen as a means of instilling terror in their slaves: their exceptionally vulnerable position fueled their exceptionally violent behavior. Less than a decade before Stedman's arrival in Surinam this vulnerability had been displayed in the Dutch colony bordering Surinam to the west. In Berbice (now part of Guiana) the slaves rebelled and destroyed Dutch power, only being subdued with the help of other Europeans and because of divisions among themselves. The Berbice slave rebellion of 1763 had been on the scale of the successful Santo Domingo revolution, which gave to slave owners the awful warning of the power of slaves.

Within Surinam for much of the eighteenth century the Dutch had had to fight a guerrilla war against Maroons, slaves who had run away from the plantations but returned to raid them, who offered an example and support to others. Ironically, the main power of these Maroons had been broken *before* Stedman's arrival in the colony. Ironically too, Surinam had by then started a long economic decline, not apparent at the time because of the amount of credit extended to planters. The final irony is that in the twentieth century in the Caribbean (but not in their Indonesian colonies) the Dutch became known as perhaps the most liberal of the imperial powers.

To return to our original question, Stedman was a fairly typical eighteenth-century soldier in his willingness to serve another country, Surinam was an economic asset that the Dutch were reluctant to lose, and the African slaves refused to be cowed by excessively brutal treatment. So Stedman arrived in Surinam to meet Joanna. . . .

PETER D. FRASER
University of London

Part One

Before Joanna

One

I, John Gabriel Stedman, was born in 1744 and from my youth have had the adventures of one many times my age. All through my intrepid youth, and indeed, far into my manhood, there have been inside me feelings tightly held by powers beyond my understanding, powers that led me sometimes to acts of the greatest generosity and concern and at other times to feats of daring and recklessness. Sometimes the sight of a beautiful woman agitated me so unreasonably that I could do naught but follow her and eventually lead her toward hours of salacious pleasure, when all duty lay forgotten.

Even though a Scotsman by birth, my own deep desire was for an artist's life in the city of Rome, where I would have indulged any number of my passions—including, of course, art—while I enjoyed to the full all the romantic escapades of men of that occupation. But alas, there being no family fortune to support such expectations, I was enlisted, at the age of twelve, as a cadet in the Scots Brigade, in which my father had also started his career. Not without protest did I follow my forebears into that dangerous profession. I pleaded to become an ensign in the British navy, but my pleas fell upon my mother's wooden ears and missed my father's altogether. Yet he loved me with a totality that often overpowered me; only after me came his other loves: the army, the English nation, and the rest of the family all in a heap.

My brother, a weak child younger than myself, was the light of my mother's life. I recall him even now, fleeing from my wrath when caught in the act of some sly misdemeanor to rest under my mother's full-flowing skirt, his screams setting the gathers astir. She loved this boy, William by name, to the utmost indulgence and felt my birth to have been a divine punishment upon her soul. She was cruel to a degree beyond the expectations of the time and blamed my father for being the cause of my ragged disposition. It is my belief, however, that it was my resentment and frustrations with my mother that caused me to express myself in dueling and fighting and, when a child, in waylaying my brother and others of his likeness.

I grew into a tall, handsome youth of Scotch and Dutch extraction. I was well-built in stature, and I cut an elegant dash in my uniform. One day in our home close to the sea at Breda in the Netherlands, Mama entertained a gaggle of women not only with sugared tea, spiced cakes, and sweetmeats, but also with extravagant stories of my rampages and ill humor in every detail. She wept into her handkerchief, allowing the cluster of women to commiserate with her, asking God's blessing upon her patience.

Almost at death's door from shame, I listened until, unable to bear more, I stripped myself to the skin and, placing my father's tricorn upon my rigid member, in which place all my anger had set, ran among the party scattering their tea. Covering their faces, they screamed in terror as I leapt into the sea, the hat now gently bobbing among the waves to my delighted singing.

"Crawford! Crawford!" my mother called to her man-servant and my tormentor. "Get him! Capture him! Bring him to me! Quick, the *spam bok* [the whip]!"

In a surge of strength I seized Crawford as he came toward me, ducking his head into the sea until, choking and sputtering, he wriggled free and fled. He had tormented me for the last time.

It was this incident that marked me in my mother's eye as a man. After deciding that I was indeed a gambler, an incessant drunkard, and an incorrigible, she gave me up as lost to her endeavors and left me free to live my life as I had chosen. She clung to my brother and held him in the vice of her love for what then seemed eternity.

I had longed for adventure ever since reading of the colonizations of the intrepid James Cook in the Pacific, not only of his conquests over the minds of natives, but also of his securing fresh lands for civilization to occupy. I was bound in my thinking, however, to the dissensions within my family.

The year of our Lord 1764 had dawned, and no one knew how it would end—whether fresh wars would break out or the enmities of old pay call. At the age of twenty I came with my regiment to Steenbergen, a small town with a small garrison, where I was united in a strong bond of friendship with George Cunninghame, a red-haired, slim young Scot with whom I visited taverns and alehouses to drink and game. I often played the fiddle while he played the fife. We were bound together in our escapades until he, having been called to the bedside of his sick father, left me at a loss for company.

In a moment of boredom I fell most desperately in love with fair Cornelia Cornel, whose father was the skipper of one of the cutters that plied up and down the river Meuse to the town of Liege, where a regiment of soldiers was quartered. Cornelia was a firmly built young woman of twenty who gave the impression of having naught but sturdy sinews, bones, and blood that became firm, well-packed pink flesh. Her dimpled young face sooner rather than later smiled at me from a heavy fall of auburn tresses, which she wore in neat braids that swung to the rhythm of her walk. One day I strode purposefully to her and, bending softly over her, kissed her tantalizingly. Unbeknown to me I was being observed by her father, who, redolent with fury, set about first to scold and then to beat me with a sturdy stick, to the merriment of the drunken assemblage who urged him on.

In the depths of shame, I returned to my lodgings. After tending the cruel welts upon my shoulder, I fell into a fitful sleep in which figured another beautiful but sensible girl, Helligonda van Calker, who often looked with smiles and pleasure in my direction.

I was still in this abysmal frame of mind when news of the death by drowning of George Cunninghame, my best friend, reached me. I wept copiously, for one whom I had known so well and who regretfully had never learned to swim. His father, who had recovered from his illness, had confirmed me a Protestant; I could but guess his grief at the loss of so worthy a son. No more the voice of dear George. No more his singing. No more his smile, his charm, his gaiety. No more his folly or his fife. Damn life! Damn death. Damn streams and rivers! I lay in bed discoursing with myself about the uncertainty of life and the certainty of death.

At that moment I heard a scratching, a whimpering, and a howling outside the door. I opened it and there sat George's pointer, whom he had called "MiLord" and who had been left at the fort. He howled; I sobbed. Then, all feeling spent, all grief expressed, he licked my face. He had become my dog and from that moment could not be separated from me. I talked to him about his master and my friend, and he understood that in waiting for the return from death one waits forever.

After a while I shifted myself from behind that curtain of gloom that had fallen over me. I went duck shooting on the sands near Flushing with Jan Van Ewe, a gaming partner. This was a treacherous place where being caught in the quicksands was greatly feared, so speedy and surprising was the coming of the tides. I had always been a strong swimmer but sometimes failed to see the dangerous nature of places and things. Sure enough, as the ducks fell to our pieces, so carried away by success were we that the tide came rapidly upon us, causing the sand to pull us down. MiLord caught me by the shoulder, and it was his skill that helped first me and then Jan to free ourselves from certain death. We watched with regret as the ducks we had meant to season and roast disappeared into the greedy sand.

Drenched, we repaired to an inn, where the innkeeper's wife took pity upon us, restoring us to full vigor with spirits, sausages, and other delicious fare. We had not long settled to rest when news reached us that Mr. Shootmaker's horse had bolted, leaving him among the shrubs and trees with a broken leg. Though damp in dress and ardor, we forsook the fire and hastened to the spot where the good man lay hurt. We found him, his cart overset and his horse rendered lame. Gently we carried him home, the sun now just past noon.

As I passed by I noticed a woman in labor in a pigsty. The pigs, in full comprehension of the proceedings, huddled at the far end of the sty, their backs to her, as they grunted in reply to her moans. I silenced MiLord, lest he should confuse the pigs, and set about to help the poor woman. By now the curious had arrived in large numbers and, believing that I was the father, began to chide me as to the proper care of my wife at such a delicate time.

"Soldiers! Bah!" they remonstrated. "Men of no conscience! It is the darkness that hides their deeds!"

"I have never seen this woman before in my life!" I pleaded.

"Say that again!" they urged.

I did. Their laughter was now even more derisive.

"It's a boy," the woman announced in an exhausted voice. "Tell me your name, sir, so that I can name my child likewise."

"Jack!" yelled Van Ewe. "Jack, I say."

"Then he too shall be called Jack," the woman answered, indicating me as an angel come from heaven.

I grew angry at the public chiding and returned to the inn in low spirits. I settled down to recall the events of the day. Jan, more comfortable with peasant folk, had not returned to the inn. Someone knocked upon the door, and thinking it was Maria, the maid who by looks and glances had declared her intentions, I invited the person to come in. The door squeaked open a little.

"Come inner and inner and inner," I teased.

Mrs. Shootmaker, the inn keeper's wife, entered, her hips now released from all but one of her petticoats to show her body to be massive in the candlelight. She lowered her eyelids. "My husband," she said coyly. "He wants help to be lifted and put straight upon the bed."

"I can't come alone, madam, but will when Jan returns. Together we will do as you require."

She smiled sadly and nodded her head.

"Madam," I queried, "do you know what became of the woman in the sty?"

"The parish took her. She was your wife?"

"No, ma'am! Before God, I had never seen the creature before in my life. I like young, pretty women."

Later that evening I connived a meeting in Maria's room and, upon returning to my own, I strayed in the darkness, fell downstairs, and woke the household to an interesting commotion. My landlady in nightcap and gown, her ample bosom heaving with rage and frustration, ordered myself and Maria out of her house as the rain poured down on every inch of earth.

"Come," said Maria without a stitch of care. "Let us go to the wine merchant's. There is everything—wine, a barn, and good straw."

We slept soundly, ate a hearty breakfast, and I returned with Jan to Steenbergen the next day.

A few weeks later, because of the exposure and the lingering and reveling in wet clothes, I became violently sick. I was greatly weakened by my illness, and upon hearing the news, my mama came to fetch me. She was an indefatigable nurse and, with the greatest care, good food, and good exercises for my mind, restored me to full health. We were reconciled, and I felt secure in her love at last.

My brother Willie had himself become a cadet and thus managed to grow in independence and stature. While I recovered from my illness he visited me many times, and we became brothers rather than adversaries. He brought me books and fanned my interest in explorers in distant lands. So struck was I by the wonders of these adventures, their scope, and the miracles of nature encountered that I spent my twenty-third birthday in a state of turmoil and anxiety. Mama wanted to see me set upon a course, and as yet there was no course set upon. Promotion in the army was slow; I was only an ensign, and the pay was not to be considered. The life of a soldier was not much removed from that of the laboring poor.

"All good men think of sons and heirs by your age, Jack," Mama said. "You have amassed nothing. We must look for an heiress for you."

Not wanting to cause a breach in the relationship with Mama, I did not contradict but agreed with her—not realizing that getting me a good wife would become her life's work.

Thoughts of adventure continued to haunt me, even though I had grown quieter in mind and devoted my time to painting, drawing, music, and riding. Instead of fantasies of beautiful women, I dwelt on nature, on poetry, and on art. I read writers such as Defoe, Hume, and Dryden, and noticed that they used the language of the day, shunning personal caprice and rejecting pedantry. I used my drawings to tell the truth about the world about me. Nature was both spectacle and story and manifested itself in many ways. Often I sat pondering the ways of nature until late into the night. The firmament was itself a most wondrous work.

One night I heard voices yelling, "Stop, thief! Stop, thief!" and then came feet thundering over the cobbles, followed by the screams and shouts and whistles of the guard. I rushed out and found the culprits to be soldiers of my regiment. The men solemnly pointed out their leader, a merry fellow called Pvt. Thomas Hoggins, who sometimes used to dance outside the alehouse to the tunes he played on his flute.

There was something in the lives of these men that I understood. The life of a fighting man was worth less than gunshot. The men were starved and beaten by people who, under the guise of religion and humanity, were capable of every cruelty. The men were often drunk and in that state committed every kind of extravagance. At this period, it must be remembered Holland was split up, partly known as the United Provinces.

"You know what will be your fate?" I asked the ringleader.

"Yes, sir," he replied. "No man cares if we live or die, we need money. Men kill for it and thieve for it. They even readily marry for it. But when they fight for it they never get paid. I know I shall be broken on the rack for this, but in time I will die of disease anyway."

The next morning I beat Hoggins and his fellows and confined them to barracks for a week. For this benevolent act the men revered me and were ready to follow me wherever I led them.

I took the men of my regiment on a long march to Deventer, another garrison town, where we were met by magistrates who bade us swear allegiance to the town. Having discoursed with others I met there as well as some who had served in the Dutch East Indies, I sent a letter to Mr. Arnoldus De Lye, a relation of my mother's who was the governor of the island of Van Ceilan (Ceylon, now Sri Lanka) in the Indian Ocean. I intimated my desire to serve abroad in the Dutch civil service and my resolution to leave the soldier's life.

The winter had nearly gone, and for all that time I had not received a letter or indeed any news of my parents. I knew that my father had been ailing and Willie, my brother, courting with the intention of getting married. One night I was told by one of the men returning from the local alehouse that the coachman at rest there carried a letter for me. I hastened there and on my way met a young man, slight in build, playful and agile in temperament, his head a mass of chestnut curls, his eyes as blue as cornflowers. There was a crowd about him, and I stopped to inquire the reason. He carried stones as big as pigeons' eggs, some indeed larger, in his hat, and from time to time he swallowed them. By shaking himself in a dance of his own concoction, the stones could be heard to rattle in his belly as they would in a sack.

He caused troubling amusement when he danced and was thought a great curiosity by the professors of Leyden, who sought to purchase his body after his death. This he revealed in a comic turn, in which he invited bystanders who had come to see him alive to be present also to see that a fair price was paid for him after his death.

When at last I reached the alehouse and accosted the coachman, I collected a letter with the black edge of mourning. My heart beat rapidly as I opened it. Alas, my poor father had died without a groan. He had borne many sorrows, many cruelties, and was a mere invalid child at the hands of my mother. He had survived the loss of his daughter to death and of his sons of life. He was found dead when thought to have been asleep.

My loss crippled me; for days I wept. My position was such that I could not afford to put myself in full mourning and so wore crepe around my arm and my sword. But the greatest mourning of all was in my heart. There lay only golden memories of my childhood talks with him, of our singing together, of his generosity and indulgence. I recalled his stories of the battles he had seen and fought, especially Fonteroy. I prayed that angels would gently place him within the walls of heaven, where he would dwell in peace.

But sadness, like a great mantle, enveloped me. My own mortality stared me in the face. If I died, none would care. I would be as a puff of air without a mark to show where I had stood. I had nothing. No money, no wife, no heir. I was a man of no substance, a shadow that had learned to parry with a sword, to knock men down, to flatter women and enjoy their flattery. I decided to resign my commission and travel to London to seek my fortune. But I had no money or any hope of any. I could not increase my indebtedness; I already owed too much.

I went about with a melancholy face, burdened by the loss of the only constant love I had known. It had often come as a gentle wind resting upon me where and when I needed its touch. My papa! Oh, my poor, dear papa! His death had set me adrift from all my hopes and intentions.

I heard his voice in my grief, saying softly, "A man must make his own chances, whether it is at gaming, cockfighting, or dueling." I was dueling with life for my life. How could I get to London, where the streets were golden pathways to fortune, and employment in the colonial service was offered in alehouses to anyone who asked? Such were the rumors that reached me over the games of card I played with men who had traveled far and wide.

I recalled many things I had done. Pretending to be Tom Jones, I had sung in the alehouses songs of my own making, mentioning all the names of the maidens I loved while throwing my lace ruffles amongst those who had come to bid us farewell as we left that post. I smirked at the simple things of my life. I had once kept a tumbler of water with a fish in it and, the weather being deuced cold, everything had become frozen, the fish so stiff that by a mere press of the hand would have broken into two. But feeling pity, I had placed it near the fire, the water melting, and it recovered its life and swam once more, showing me how firm was the life in the body of living things. Were its sensations those that I now felt, I pondered long and well. What did it feel? That poor fish! I recalled also dancing a minuet with a whore upon the ice and, being exceedingly drunk, falling into a hole. I was ready to freeze, but MiLord saved me by means of a rope tied to his collar. He had drawn me to safety then and in the same manner used to draw me through the streets in the moonshine at above sixteen miles an hour, the bells upon his collar tinkling merry notes.

All these thoughts compelled me to recall my dog, MiLord, that my illness at Steenbergen had caused me to entrust to the loving care of friends. My heart was indeed heavy with concern for him. Was he still alive or had he too gone? I wept again for two that I deeply loved.

Amongst these reflections, some sad, some amusing, I began to ponder my legacy and the use to which I could put whatever goods my father had left me. There were several books, a map of the earth, a silver penknife, and a silver St. Andrew's cross. The two last I resolved to keep to the end of my days. The books, some encompassing the works of the great thinkers of the day and one the pictures and prints of Mr. William Hogarth, I decided to auction and with the money go to London. My father had meticulously collected prints few people called art and many described as scurrilous. He loved particularly the works of Mr. Hogarth. Noticing my inclination to act hastily, he had often, as if in warning, drawn my attention to Mr. Hogarth's dissolute family pictures, in which he used either dogs or children to parody the pompous adults of the time. He also used fallen women and the young of the indigent as forms of decoration to question the established order.

My father had said that the great man had been imprisoned as a child of eleven and confined for five years and so understood the feelings he portrayed in his art. My father, being a jocular man himself, saw Mr. Hogarth's use of innocent children to add a tinge of disorder to pomposity and to parody self-importance as actions of great consequence.

There was also among my store *Emile*, a book Jean-Jacques Rousseau had written with much feeling, although it had been rumored that a child found in the basket at the Foundling Hospital had been his child of the book *Emile*. Since my father had been, in his healthier days, a great raconteur, I felt that his spirit remained forever a part of his books, especially one of William Blake's and the Rousseau. Those two, I decided, I would keep. In his beautiful hand my father had written a few lines from a "song" of Mr. Blake's:

And when night comes I'll go
To places fit for Woe.
Walking along the darkened valley
With silent melancholy.

I planned the auction with some care, inviting all the officers to my room one morning following parade. When they had gathered, I spoke with great sincerity about the virtues of my father. I then placed a bottle of gin and some snuff upon the table and chose a captain of another battalion to be the auctioneer, who would sell to the highest bidders all my father's books. For the whole I raised above ten pounds sterling, and so I was set on my tracks for London.

Full of news, I sought my pretty Helligonda and took a lock of her hair, giving her mine in return. We spoke of our love and of our poverty.

"You can have money, too, Jack. I shall tell my parents naught but the truth of my love for you."

15

"That will not please them, being Anabaptists!" said I. "And I a mere dancing Protestant who believes that we are all born in sin."

"Nevertheless, it is my heart. And I must take care of it," she protested.

She did tell them of our love and, amidst tears of unhappiness, was debarred my presence. Her father demanded that we return each other's letters. Upon satisfying that expectation, I solemnly took my last embrace of her. She gave me a letter of introduction to Sir Clifton Wintringham, with whom she had stayed in London, and also managed to slip into the pocket of my coat several florins, which, not knowing of their existence, I could not return to her. I said farewell to my many friends and, in the guise of a common sailor, hove anchor for London.

What can I say about the voyage except that it was tedious, confining, and rough? I was doubly confined, first to a cabin of no consequence and second to the disguise of a common sailor among other sailors—vagabonds, thieves, and scoundrels, most of whom life at sea had rid of every grain of decency and good conduct.

We sailed under English colors and on the first day made good headway, with a fair sky and a heaving sea. We then encountered another Indiaman coming home. It looked weatherworn. When not far alongside, we could see the troops in the tattered, faded jackets that had once been whole and scarlet; the faces of the crew, even at a distance, seemed work-worn and sad. Our captain exchanged greetings, and we passed on.

The women of quality on board would not exchange pleasantries with a common sailor who knew that for far too long he had indulged himself with women of low virtue. So I read my Bible as well as the *Songs of Mr. Blake* to pass the days away.

In the morning the sea was low and calm and the wind fair and light, but toward evening a fog bank rose on the horizon. To present myself as a true sailor, I swept the horizon to the eastward after climbing the rigging. To my surprise I saw a lugger with a mast that had no sails set yet flew the pirate's flag. She seemed a large lugger, and hurrying down to the poop, I informed the crew of my observations and added that she would try to take us by surprise when the blanket of fog had fattened and spread, since she flew the pirate's flag.

The captain thought for a while and then said, "She is waiting for the fog to roll down with a shift in the wind, and then she will try to get alongside."

We had women on board, one with two children, and those we decided to set in safety. But the women would not hear of it, offering to stay aft to take care of the wounded, to hand up muskets and ammunitions, and to do whatever fell to necessity. The children we set in perfect safety.

The officers kept watch on the lugger, and then, with a suddenness that only sailors know, the fog came rolling down on us, thickening like soup and so shielding us.

"Who are they?" we whispered.

"Privateers! And French they must be, in these waters."

"The cowards! Lock up the Frenchman on board!" A pair of our men hurried to comply.

We waited with beating hearts, anticipating bloodshed and mutilation. Time crawled, and then we saw it: a sail on our lee quarter, not half a cable-length away. Our captain ordered our men to come up in silence. But the lugger was now alongside, banging against our mizzen chains as she rolled with the swell. The men aboard were pirates—white men and Negroes. Biting on their knives, they lost no time trying to scamper up the side, screeching and hacking at the ropes. We repulsed them with our bayonets, but they came at us again. Showering them with shot, we were for a time rid of them; but that was not to be for long. They came back at us until, with prolonged shooting, we quelled their guns and their hacking of our ropes.

When all was quiet, our men slipped down the rigging and found in the lugger ten men dead but much booty, which our captain confiscated to be handed over when we berthed. We scuttled the lugger before resuming our journey.

There was much merriment on board. The French passenger was released with apologies from confinement. Without further anxieties, a fiddle being found, we danced upon the deck.

Free from further apprehension, we passed other ships. By gaming with anyone who was willing I enhanced my fortune by another five guineas. I came out of my disguise on the day before we docked. Seeing how much less people regarded a common British sailor than an ensign in a foreign army, I decided that each had some usage at the correct time. I became an ensign, the lowest commissioned officer, again, with fifteen guineas and the five florins in my pocket that Helligonda had secreted upon my person. We had crossed the English Channel in one week and ten hours.

I smelled London—the land and the river Thames—before I saw it. There was a fog about, giving the idea of vagueness. The trees were silhouettes; the people dissolved as we waited on board. Then suddenly the sun broke through as if by magic. Everything emerged: bridges, dogs, water, everything.

We docked close to Greenwich, the passengers scurrying up the landing stairs set all along the river. The sun's rays fell upon the gently undulating river, enhancing the shapes and sizes of the flotsam and jetsam. Cargo ships unloaded goods from all over the globe, and the river pirates and watermen were in gleeful mood at being able to thieve and conceal with impunity. Craft of many sizes and variety sat in the lap and pull of the river: spritsail barges with tall masts, luggers, frigates, tugs, merchantmen all with the stains of travel about their bows. Moored boats tossed about in the traffic of men shouting and whistling.

I had come out into the labyrinth of the docks, into the swirl and rush of humanity in a myriad of shades and faces. I was being swept past stalls of all kinds: street sellers, beggars, rogues, and flower sellers. Church spires towered above me with the rattles of cranes and derricks beyond me.

"What is this place?" I asked.

"Rotten Row, good sir."

"Where can I find an alehouse?"

"Use your eyes to take notice of the bridge. There's one beyond."

I walked along, my bag a burden, to a dejected row of buildings huddled close like fish that had been beached. In the distance were even more ships, rust-eaten, grimy, and forgotten. They matched the beachcombers who awaited opportunity for roguery by sneaking off with goods. Decay and despair encircled the docks like a merciless chain. I called a hackney coach and bade the coachman take me to an inn where I would do well for a night or two before finding lodgings. The horse trotted wearily along the cobbled streets.

So this was London! A city I could never have imagined in full detail. I was almost overcome by the sound and the stench. Even inside the coach I was assailed by ribaldry and curses intermingling with the choruses of people crying their wares.

I was taken to the Black Lion Inn, where the noise and glare continued to fatigue me. I dined on bread and cheese, washed and shaved and drank the health of my landord, a stocky, clean-shaven, and merry fellow, and went to bed. On the morrow his wife, a good woman, entertained me with talk and told me the location of a sound, safe lodging house. I had exactly the fifteen pounds and four florins with which, informed the landlord amicably, I could live in, although not a fashionable part, a good part of the town. I rented a small dining room and bedchamber that were sufficient for my needs at the cost of two shillings a week, to include my bed linen.

On going through my belongings that night I came upon a letter Pvt. Tommy Hoggins had asked me to send or take to his mother. Later that week I traveled to the address and it being Saturday, came upon a market there. On walking farther my nose was full of an acrid odor that permeated the whole place, rendering it sharp, damp, stinging yet pungent. It was the smell of blood from the abattoirs where the cows were killed. It was a terrible perfume, for a river of blood flowed quietly, perpetually, into the street and the drains. I entered a world where on one side stood the living beasts and on the other the dying. I glimpsed those who skinned the steaming carcasses.

There were two weapons of slaughter, the poleax of the Christians and the swift Jewish knife, the *shochet*, that never bungled. I was stunned by this horror, but managed to watch as the meat was searched for disease, the slightest hint of which condemned it.

As I emerged I felt hungry, although my stomach was overthrown. A hawker sold strange fruit. Women with red, puffed cheeks, dull eyes, and oily hair bandied jests with loafers and onlookers. I entered the King of Denmark Tavern and after a pint of ale went into the street behind an alehouse and knocked on the door of no. 8. There was a sign that read: "Hoggins, Maker and Mender of Wigs" across the door.

The room I entered was full of human hair of all colors and lengths. In the dim light a man of a seemly disposition worked as though under a spell. He never looked up once. But there were wigs of all kinds and fashions guarded by two girls. One was about fourteen, small for her age and yet of good color, who busied herself. The other, younger by about seven years, clutched a homemade baby doll and a whistle she said she blew when pilferers came so that the guard might attend them.

I introduced myself and inquired after Mrs. Hoggins. The husband quietly continued to work, reluctant even to shift his eyes for a single minute.

"Ma be sick. She be in Bethlehem Hospital. They say she be a lunatic, but she ain't none o' that," informed the older girl.

"Can I see your mother then? Tom said to be certain this letter was given to none but her."

"Go there, sir, any Sunday afternoon. You could see her for a penny or two, good sir."

I took my leave and, calling a coach, I journeyed to Dolly's Steak House, where my landlady had informed me many great men met to talk while indulging in good, cheap eating. My vanity had got the better of me, and so I sat down to dinner in this place of much fame.

21

No man instructed me where I should sit, for such was the custom to sit wherever there was a place. The room was cozy and comfortable, and my beefsteak was cleverly done, causing me to forget the abattoir. Bread, beef, and beer all served by a waiter for a single penny caused me to spend just one shilling, and I was even allowed gingerbread and apples to treat myself with later.

I did not go home, but went into an alehouse and sat down among scoundrels and loafers to drink some beer. They urged me to go cockfighting to the pit close by, where the seats were covered with coarse matting. The cocks were finely dressed and armed with spurs to fight with. The noise of the betting was an uproar in my ears as the cocks fought. Win, lose, or die, the mental torture of the betting fraternity was similar to the torment of the poor fighting cocks. Later, the night being pitch dark, I hired a linkboy to precede me with a flaming torch all the way home.

My lodging proved to be too quiet for me. I needed the company of young people and took fresh lodgings in St. Martin's Lane, close to which there were green fields and a fine church. There I had a small room but much access to eating houses. The prices of hackney coaches caused money to fly the purse, although walking had caused me no objection and indeed had often been a source of great pleasure to me, especially in the early dawn when I drew the houses and places that took my fancy.

After my change of abode I came upon Patrasso, a Negro, in the following manner: Being again much bothered and haunted by memories of my father, I sought to find peace at St. Martin's Church, where I heard a good sermon on the blessings of piety by Mr. Granville Sharp, abolitionist and avowed friend of the slaves in captivity in the Caribbean colonies. After the service the congregation, consisting of some Negroes, gathered to tell their stories and to pay their respects at the graveside of one Thomas Smith, a Christian slave who had died from years of ill usage. Several of the Negroes had by various means obtained their freedom and showed their desire to win for their fellows that same state. Some were bedraggled, but others wore fine clothes. Patrasso, a rawboned, gleaming, one-armed giant, sold muffins every day except Sunday. His voice, a fine baritone, caused the singing to become a celebration to the Almighty.

His master had fallen into the river, and he had jumped right in to save him. He had seized his master's clothing, but the current, being stronger than he, swept his master away. His distraught mistress had his hand amputated for his negligence. He told his story with piety and without any matter of anger whatsoever.

Besides Patrasso there was Gronniosaw, who also told his story.

"My mother," he said, "was the eldest daughter of the King of Zarra. I was the youngest of six. An ivory merchant, after stealing me, sold me for two yards of check cloth. I was sold many times more. Upon my obtaining my freedom after the death of my mistress I was left destitute and friendless and after much persuasion joined an expedition of privateers who cheated me of my share of money. I then enlisted in the North Gloucestershire Regiment and, upon receiving my discharge, came to England. In London I married Betty, a weaver I found living hard. For years she had been a poor widow with a child. We moved to Colchester, but work was hard to come by. We were reduced to the greatest distress, but finally God was on our side and saved us. I know, as all blacks know, the rattling of chains, the crack of whips, and the groans and cries of my brethren."

I gave him a shilling and thanked him for acquainting me with his history.

That afternoon I visited the King's Picture Gallery. The contrast between those replicas that looked dreamily out of thick gilt frames at us and the solid, fastidious living was so great as to be burdensome. I admired the languorous beauty of the court maidens and matrons decked in finery of fur and feather, silks and satins, their voluptuous hips and sleepy eyes speaking of sensuality unspent. Time had not tumbled their hair even after all the centuries that had passed, and tendrils still beguiled me as they wandered over pale white brow or rose-tinted cheeks. I lost my heart to duchesses and countesses, courtesans and simple women, and asked myself who were these women with such subtle faces and quiet, mysterious eyes and who wore such lavish ornaments of diamonds and pearls around their stately necks? I did not consider the men, for it was not pleasing to place a garland of flowers with tenderness and desire upon the brow of a man. It was indeed a difficult thing to regard all these people of such elaborate unreality as having lived on God's earth at all. There were black servants in many of the pictures, and this made me keen to notice people of different races. I spoke to two smiling Chinamen and bought some strange concoction they said was made of very fine rice. I spoke to Gypsies, too, and upon seeing one outside an alehouse where none would serve him, I carried out a jug of beer to him.

I took an early walk to St. James' Park on the following day and stopped to see the guards on parade. There were beautiful women—real ones this time—and I thought with much longing of my loving Anabaptist, Helligonda. I then walked to St Paul's and, the day being cold, I dined on a thick pea soup with slices of ham and good bread and then on fish with butter sauce, potatoes, cabbage, and apple pie. I sat to a good helping and fell into conversation with a tall, stately gentleman who offered to enlist me in the Grenadier Guards. My heart was still set upon travel, however, and after drinking a jug of beer in a gulp he introduced himself as a man of consequence, George Dempster Esq. by name, and a politician and lawyer. He seemed to be a solid man in every respect and invited me the very next day to breakfast with him and his sister, who tended his house. It was a charming visit, his sister an older woman indulgent and concerned for my well-being.

My funds were getting exceptionally low, but I did not curtail my visits to the Tower of London, Vauxhall, Hyde Park, and other places of interest.

Realizing that I must soon succeed in my enterprise or return to the army, I took Helligonda's letter of introduction and called upon Sir Clifton and Lady Wintringham, who made me welcome and invited me to visit the playhouse to see *The Merry Wives of Windsor*. We took very good seats, not quite at the spikes* but good enough for all we saw and heard to be distinct. We walked in St James' Park, where there were wildfowl in great numbers, and we saw the footguards in drill and parade. We talked pleasantly about life in Holland, and it was clear that Sir Clifton had come away from it happily and without regret.

Upon leaving them, I thought that being nearly six months away, the time to do or die had come. I decided

---

*The front row.

that a half-month longer was all that I would allow myself.

I resumed my sailor's garb and followed the throng of people to Nightingale Lane, where birds of every kind could be bought. The chirrupings, flutings, cawings, and singing could be heard for miles. The sale of these poor creatures was a sad show, and while engaging a young bird seller in talk I released his stock of canaries to sing their tunes as nature willed, while reciting my own composition, "To Dead Larks." I offered the man ten shillings for his load, but he demanded more. An audience gathering around me, I set down my hat upturned to receive a penny paid for the pleasure of one of my poems, which I recited again in a merry manner. My hat collected two shillings and three pence farthing for this woeful sermon, and adding to it the ten shillings, I thought him well paid.

It is best, when in London, to follow the tide of humanity and rest where washed up. I had been now some time without female sport and was unhappy in this respect about my situation. One day, close to London Tower, where I had gone to view the Crown Jewels, I came upon Rosie Jude, whose father was a sailmaker. She was a young woman of some fashion, tall and fair-haired, with a figure that accommodated her clothes. We walked to Vauxhall and had a merry time together.

She was an agreeable soul; but when I tried to kiss her she parried and said, "Sir, I am sure, sir, that if I am to be familiar with a gentleman, I should rather choose my betrothed, a substantial man unworthy of such betrayal."

"I am certain, madam," said I, "that I too would like to be in a similar position." I gave some indication of being wounded by her words.

"You are leading me into a strange confusion, sir. I hope we could get better acquainted in that respect upon another occasion."

"What I like best, Mistress Rosie, is an agreeable female companion. That is all."

So we walked arm in arm to Newgate, where a hanging was to take place. Mistress Rosie continued to tell me about her choicest memories. "My father saw with his own two eyes when wicked Hannah Diego, the thief and vagabond, struck the executioner before he chopped her head off. A big woman she was and strong. Went to her Maker in a hale of swearing and even asked the devil to take her."

Mistress Rosie knew all the niceties of that terrible place, and I hoped by my show of interest to bring her round to sup with me. But she continued to be first with both ancient and recent news. "That black slave James Somerset, 'ave you heard of 'im? His former master had got the hold of 'im to take 'im back to Jamaica to make a slave of 'im once more. But the Lord Justice loosed 'is bonds and set 'im free. 'Aven't you 'eared?"

We drank tea at a tea shop on the way back, and then I kissed her hand and we went our separate ways. I picked up a seemingly fashionable lady in the Strand and toyed with her for five shillings.

The errand Tom Hoggins had so faithfully asked me to undertake still lay heavily upon my mind. I went to church at St. Paul's and enjoyed the choir singing and after went to Bethlehem Hospital, still refreshed with the Word of God. I had seen many horrifying sights, mainly among the poor of London, but this was the most horrendous of all. Mrs. Hoggins, like many other people, wore her name around her neck, and a hundred people of all ages, at least having paid two pence apiece, went into the ward to make sport of the lunatics in their utmost misery. Some of the mob provoked them into a rage, poor wretches, while others laughed at their ravings.

I could not get close to Mrs. Hoggins to talk to her, but in a gesture of generosity and a voice full of audacity's essence she yelled, "This be gold from my Tommy. He be a rich man of gold in the Indies." And she threw nothing yet something of great value at the rabble who fairly trampled upon her.

That night I took stock of my situation. In London, wealth and influence were what made men succeed. I had neither. It was clear that those I had met were men of words and not of deeds. I visited East India House, the Head Office of the East India Company, in person and stood beneath the portraits of the great statesmen of the day. I waited for someone to educate or even enlighten me on how to secure a position in the world beyond.

Instead, a gray-haired scribe, himself almost covered with books and paper, saw me and asked, "Are you, sir, the new clerk now come from the Custom House? I need a helper. There is much to be done."

"No, sir, I am not he," I said. "But I vow to give an honest man's toil for a good day's wages."

"How many days can you work at counting the boxes of tea unloaded from the barges on the river?"

"One," I said, holding up a finger. "I will return to my home in Holland tomorrow on the packet to Bayonne. I have but one guinea and one half-crown left of all my inheritance in the world."

He smiled and set me to counting hogsheads of sugar instead. I worked until five o'clock and missed the sailing to Bayonne, but earned a shilling for my tallying. I could have stayed there to work, but two voices called—Mama's and my sweet Helligonda's.

I spent my last night in London at a party given for the christening of Harold, a freed black who was much admired for his knowledge of mathematics and music. A group of people had gathered in the church to watch the act that conferred upon Harold a soul, which as a black he was not born with and which would come with reclamation from slavery. It was a fine occasion, and Harold, relieved, went off with his benefactor, a stalwart and convinced abolitionist.

My landlord was sorry, he said, to see me go, but I had seen the great metropolis, and truly worthy to be called great it was. The sight of it had uplifted my heart, and now there was sadness. I walked to the Westminster, meaning to go by boat to Greenwich pier, at the same time taking my last look about me. All along the street the tide of people flowed. London was at its worst that day—the stench and noise of voices, unshod horses, and loafers loudly bantering and hailing others of their kind in every direction rang too vividly upon my ears. And so, hailing a cab, I journeyed to Greenwich pier from where the vessel was to sail next day at dusk. I had but a single guinea, a florin, and a sixpence standing betwixt myself and beggary. A journey lay before me, yet I must spend another night on land.

Then a thought struck me. The sailmaker, Mr. Jude—I could pay him my respects and ask him most kindly to convey similar respects to Rosie, his sumptuous daughter. There were men about him when I called at his yard where, with three apprentice lads, he made and mended sails. It was noon, and after talking with him most heartily, I offered him to dine with me somewhere close.

"I know a fair place," said he. "The John Bull. It is a comely place and clean, and my little varlet might well be there, as she leaves the milliner's at this hour. She is a fine milliner, is Rosie, and hobnobs on this account with many grand ladies."

We sat to a meal of bread, cheese, and ale. Before the eating was complete, in walked his little varlet, as lovely as ever and in as high a fashion as would unsettle titled ladies.

"Mistress Rosie!" I exclaimed. "It fills my heart with pleasure to see one so pretty this day."

She sat with us, listened to my predicament, and, with her father's permission, invited me to drink tea and to stay until such time as it was prudent to board my ship. Not knowing that her betrothed did not exist, I envied him beyond any man until, the flesh and the devil taking hold of me, I kissed her. She allowed me to speak of my desire for her and finally consented to my attentions. I whispered into her ear. "Tell me, Mistress Rosie, how many petticoats do you wear?"

And she, in as ribald a manner, replied, "Two or three, dear sir, and then there is the best one of all. Let's play Blind Man's Buff."

And so we did, all around the bed like a mountain in the room.

She possessed a most sensuous and shapely form, since nature, in a capricious mood, had made her capricious. Her dainty golden head and delicately smooth shoulders delighted me, and when she kissed me I was swept out of the land of things as they were into the land of things as they were not. Her breath was the fragrance of folly. One by one the lights of resistance were dimmed. Pierrot and Pirette were dreams, and time was but the tomb of dreams; and desire, like a string of fireflies, showed us the way to ecstasy.

We took tea and I journeyed once more to acquaint myself with the hour of sailing. It was still the same, and so once more I walked with Rosie in Kensington Gardens. Thrush and blackbird were singing, and through the branches the wind and the evening sun played on the water in the pond. Near its edges sheep nibbled the herbage and dipped their soft noses into the water. Overhead birds were hurrying home to roost. Rooks cawed eagerly and sparrows rose in flight at our intrusion. The shadows lengthened as we smiled tenderly at each other. It began to rain and we started back as we had come. The taverns we passed were crowded with rough men. Sightseers dragged tired children home over cobbles slimy with rain. I looked at the feet before me. They were a nightmare! Feet in boots of all colors, hideous boots trodden out of shape, high-heeled boots, mud- and slush-soaked boots, and those of the walking living and the walking dead.

I hurried down to the pier. The tide was running fast, and we parted immediately. A beggar played a melody upon his flute. A woman wailed "Drink to Me Only with Thine Eyes" while I grappled with the foul reek of the river. I was returning to the old familiar faces and tried to comfort myself with the remembrances of London, its lonely face and its lonely pleasures—except for Rosie, who brightened the gloom of my gaiety and the darkness of my amusements.

"Adieu, Mistress Rosie!" I called.

She grew smaller and smaller in the distance, but she was larger and stronger in my heart.

This was the Age of Reason, but there had been no reason among the common man in London, the poor not able to imagine a thought other than their own and believing the gentry to be a species far beyond their call and reach. The poor accepted a simple life of drinking, gambling, work perhaps, sport maybe, and a good hanging providing flashes of color to excite and delight them.

I now felt exhausted and weather-worn, this coming firmly to me on the uneventful journey to Rotherham, where, after a restful period with moderate excitement and a pretty girl to supper, I took passage to Nijmegen in Holland. I called upon my friends and there found MiLord in good health. But alas, his loyalty had gone from me, although he recognized me and was playful. I stroked him and presented an apple, which he had loved to munch and was now disdainful toward. I took my leave. I bade them all long lives and journeyed to my regiment.

The prodigal son had returned—once again to the life of stern discipline, warm drill, and cold guard duty, where I had often sung and played my fife to keep my spirits alive, soothed the hearts of lovelorn maids, and watched the antics of the night-walkers.

Although so low in my own self-control, I had sometimes to drill the men, bastinading* deserters and beating and reprimanding the shirkers. Regiments were often bought and sold with easy intention, and I had once more returned to all the colors and seasons of the soldier's life. *What now?* I thought. *What now that I am back with my old regiment?*

---

*Beating on the soles of the feet.

Part Two

Joanna, My Love, My Life

Two

I reported to the honorable Gen. John Stuart, a man of fine parts who was much respected as a competent and fearless soldier. He welcomed me heartily, first as the prodigal son of the regiment, then as a Scotsman like himself. Afterward, over a dram of whiskey, he suggested that I regale the corps with an account of my visit to London, the cosmopolis of the world.

I could not adequately give account of the din of the dockyards or the stench of drains and abattoirs, for I could recall no smell like those, nor of the debris of the streets nor the stark and shameless poverty of the poor. I tried as vividly as I could to describe the clatter of the hooves of the horses on the cobblestones and the cries of the people being pilloried or publicly whipped. The purposes of those moving as a flow hither and thither, as well as their ribaldry and merriment at a hanging at Tyburn or Newgate, all confounded me sorely. The soldiers appreciated these descriptions so hugely that in the pleasure of the moment I almost forgot to introduce my drawings of the fashionable houses of famous Londoners, a task I had undertaken on my early-morning meanderings through the streets.

I found it saddening that my journey had not stretched farther—beyond oceans and seas to adventures and sights I could not imagine—and I hoped that one day I would go farther into the unknown, although I had failed in my endeavors to reach the Dutch East Indies.

"Look to Surinam, Ensign Stedman. There's trouble brewing in that colony!" said our general. "The slaves have revolted and have been destructive and barbarous, as only heathens can be, to their true and rightful owners."

I began to acquaint myself with the facts about the matter, since Surinam was a Dutch colony in that vast land of Guiana.

At that time I was called to the Hague to attend court and wait on His Highness the Prince of Orange. It was a happy time for me. I lived in the utmost comfort and rode, gamed, and danced in the company of desirable women. But there were mounting rumors about the rebels and the companies of mercenaries that were being bought and sold in the expectation of war in Surinam in Dutch Guiana on the coast of South America. At that time the Dutch nation was reputed to be the most barbarous in its suppression of the slaves, who grossly outnumbered whites on their plantations in the New World.

In fact, the slaves had never previously risen in open rebellion but had escaped in ever-increasing numbers to the inland forests. From the earliest days of slavery they set up settlements and returned in the dead of night to plunder, hack their tormentors to death, and set the torch to their former owners' possessions. Whites fled their plantations in the wake of destruction and failed enterprise, while more deserters swelled the numbers of bush Negroes. The Amsterdam market caught a chill, developed a fever, and eventually suspended ready credit for investment in Surinam. But the slaves paid for the planters' losses in the form of mortal beatings, live burnings, summary drownings of infants, and other bizarre forms of torture. It was even reported that the women of the

36

Dutch nation excelled the men in the design and application of torment upon the helpless! In 1749, 1760, and 1762 the Surinamese concluded peace treaties with the slaves, since all attempts to destroy them had failed.

The civilized nations closed ranks, and soldiers from the dregs of society volunteered against the heathens, who found themselves with new owners and even more devilish overseers as the plantations changed hands. These plantations had first and foremost been attempts at increasing Dutch wealth by using Amerindian slaves to grow cocoa, coffee, tobacco, and sugar. These slaves had died of overwork and ill-usage, thus leading over the next century to black chattel slavery.

An expedition to Surinam under Capt. Louis Henry Fourgeoud was mounted. The Prince of Orange appointed him colonel and myself captain, and I volunteered to join his company of men. After swearing the oath of loyalty to the Prince, I hastened home, traveling night and day on horseback to say farewell to friends and family. I was not going to a conventional war but to guerrilla warfare in the jungles of Surinam, chasing rebels from site to site in an effort to corrode their resistance.

I found my mother resigned to the loss of my father and more indulgent in her opinions about me. She seemed troubled about the expedition, as prior to her marriage she had traveled to Plantation Charity in Paramaribo, Surinam, which her Uncle Reygersman then owned.

"It was a wicked place," she told me. "The whole colony was without God but had kirks aplenty. My Aunt Hilde did not spare her slaves. Why, she drowned a baby for crying too loudly. And if the slaves had too many brats, she threw them into the river after picking out the sturdiest. She was the devil's daughter, my Aunt Hilde!"

It made me think. Did cruel people own slaves, or did the institution of slavery breed cruelty?

I understood my mother's nature better after that, and I was delighted when she showed some unaccustomed humanity and gave me a box of commodities for my journey. My brother, too, had matured; leaving my mother to his capable and devoted care, I returned and placed myself at Colonel Fourgeoud's service.

I found that he was already in confrontation with Jean Nepveu, a man more of sense than of learning who had risen from sweeping the hall of the courthouse to his position as commander of the Society Troops. He had accumulated a fortune by quiet endeavors and commanded respect from all ranks of people, no one daring to attack him but at a distance. His deportment was affable but ironical, and he was always in full command of his temper; he gave the appearance of a man of fashion and influence. His nickname was "Reynard" because he cleverly outfoxed the hounds of the colony of Surinam who were ever trying to destroy him.

Colonel Fourgeoud was, on the other hand, tempestuous, passionate, self-sufficient, and vengeful. He was not cruel to individuals, but was a tyrant in general. Later, after he had sent many men to their deaths, I was to know him as avaricious, oppressive, committed, and indefatigable. He was also heroic in certain circumstances.

I remained neutral in the clash between the two. Nepveu, by talking better, forced Fourgeoud to act worse.

It was only when we were out at sea that the old shaver revealed the true colors of his nature. The colonel disregarded weakness, illness, or any show of an indifferent constitution in the men. He was so relentless at times that even Captain Hesseling, who had slung his hammock next to mine and was genuinely showing all the signs of the smallpox, was refused permission to seek treatment ashore.

The young man was in such a state that the men protested and argued among themselves so strongly that Fourgeoud relented. He, however, blamed me, commented derogatorily upon my clothes, and ordered me aboard the frigate *Zeelust* with Capt. John Reims and Major Westerloo.

The colonel, now in a churlish state of vengeance, gave orders that all our fresh fruits and vegetables on board the ships were to be locked away; he ordered also that we eat without complaint salted fish, pork, and beef at every meal. Not being used to the effects of salt, our stomachs fulminated against it; I was only restored to good health by a dosage of ivory and brimstone, which my mother swore to be unfailing in its effects for good upon the constitution.

But the next day fate intervened. A fresh gale rose and forced us to batten down the hatches fore and aft to keep out the foaming sea. The ship tossed and turned in the gale, the cargo rolling around like marbles. The poor animals either broke their legs or were mortally injured, so allowing us, by their untimely deaths, the fresh meat for which we had grown desperate. And thus the journey continued: here windbound, there a gale, with good sea and weather on those days when Fate smiled upon us.

For days all was well, with a clear sky, the wind in our favor, and the sea running fair. We had now passed the tropics, and a melancholy descended upon me. Helligonda came back into my mind as if to emphasize the expanse of sea and sky which now lay between us. Standing on deck, I reread all the letters that had been returned to me, ceremonially destroyed them, and threw them over the side with the lock of her hair. And she was thus swept away out of my mind and my life.

That day the run of the frigate through the water, with its back to the wind, was fast and free; all around us spread the sky with its fleece of clouds and before us the wide expanse of sea, until suddenly we came to a river branching into sweeps of verdure. It was the Surinam River, about four miles wide—the end of the spread of Dutch territories along the Atlantic Ocean from Cape Nassau to Marowijna, to include the Essequibo River, the Demerara River, the Berbice River, and the Surinam, as well as the Courentyne, the Coppename, the Saramacca, and the Marowijna. The whole area was held under Guiana, although separately governed. The colony of Surinam arose along the coastline from the cultivation of the banks of the rivers, looking like the painting of an old master.

We dropped anchor at Fort Zeelandia a few miles from the ports of Paramaribo, where people greeted us and cheered until we went briefly ashore before journeying to the town itself. Paramaribo seemed a very lively place, the streets crowded with planters, sailors, Jews, Indians, and Africans while the river played host to tent barges rowed by stalwart Africans. Merchants and their families in truly magnificent dress of Genoa velvets, silk embroidery, diamonds, and gold and silver lace exposed their wealth. But nothing showed wealth more than the number of slaves that attended the planters. The town was well supplied with provisions, but housing was expensive. The ladies' dresses reflected their elegance, but they were known to be stern mistresses of their elaborate households.

After the official ceremonies were over, we marched with bagpipe and drum to our quarters. That very night all were invited to dine at the governor's table. Several of the men had fallen sick on board, their teeth loose from the scurvy, but they managed to attend after the services of a physician had been procured for them.

What a banquet it was after sixty-three days at sea! We were served by beautiful slaves of color varying from black to white tinged with golden sunlight. They attended to our every need as was expected of them, so little choice of thought, action, or intention had they.

Afterward, I walked alone through the streets to seek out the dwelling of a wealthy planter named Lolkens, who had offered to accommodate me until I could arrange my own particulars. Upon calling there I found the house in darkness, but being sorely in need of rest, I kept up the knocking.

Eventually a slave girl, fairly masculine in appearance, opened the door. She was so friendly that I was frightened by her eagerness to embrace me and engage in certain intimacies upon my person.

"Mr. Lolkens," she said, "has gone to visit his plantation." All the while she grew more desperate in her intentions. I resisted and she commenced to jabber and to weep. In order to explain her tears, she turned round and showed me the whip scars on her back.

I patted her arm, indicating that I was not displeased with her but was tired and wanted to sleep. Mustering her strength, she pushed me down upon the bed and undressed me, as was her duty. In the end, the flesh and the devil got the better of me.

Lolkens returned the next day. Upon questioning me closely about the frightened girl, he was satisfied with my description of her as willing and obliging.

41

A week later I had established myself in my own house, which the wives of my many friends had liberally and tastefully furnished for me. I had not, however, managed to arrange satisfactorily for my food to be prepared, so I dined with the Lolkens family and breakfasted with the Joshua Demellys, she a charming lady and he secretary to the Court of Policy. Sometimes I went to visit the Kennedys, who had a fine little four-year-old boy. He looked so charming in his velvet dresses that this I found endearing to my need one day of a child of my own.

There were many slaves at the Demellys'—beautiful women with finely chiseled features, women whom white men and black women had created and re-created through the centuries to the point of wonder. But I had shared so many blissful moments with women of culture, elegance, and sophistication that these slave girls meant no more than momentary pleasure to me and were of no more interest than the exotic birds and other creatures in the colony.

And then one day it all changed. A silent drama took place, with me in the character of a desperate lover.

I had breakfasted at the Demellys' and had taken a few moments to indulge in conversation with the lady of the house when a young mixed-race girl, no more than fifteen, entered the room in attendance upon her mistress, a large, sad lady by the name of Mrs. DuBois. The girl's perfection of face and form startled me. There was music and all the light and shade of poetry in her movements. My eyes followed her around the room with the utmost compulsion. She lowered her gaze modestly, but we knew that my heart had spoken and hers had heard. She tended her mistress with a delicate devotion and smiled with the greatest circumspection.

"Who is that girl?" I asked Mrs. Demelly.

"Joanna," she said. "A great favorite with us all. And she is in fact a slave girl."

"Favorite! Bah! Only yesterday I saw Miss Stolker's favorite dying of the beating she received on her bare buttocks!" I replied.

"Well, sir, the Stolkers make a special compote of their cruelty. They will get their reward in good time, I do believe that most firmly, and I can assure you it will not be sweet."

"What do you know of Joanna? Be so kind as to tell me!"

"Only if you play me a Mozart sonata upon your violin, Mr. Stedman."

"I will after you have told me," I promised.

"She is, sir," said Mrs. Demelly, "the daughter of a respectable gentleman named Kruythoff, a man of culture and learning who had, besides this girl, four children by an African woman called Cery, the property of Mr. DuBois on his estate, Fauconberg, in the upper part of the river Comewina. In Surinam all children go with their mothers and belong to their master unless the father obtains them by purchase. Some few years since, Mr. Kruythoff made the offer of over a thousand pounds to obtain manumission for his family, which being inhumanely refused he became frantic and died in that melancholy state soon after, leaving in slavery at the hands of a tyrant his five children, the eldest of whom is Joanna."

"And where is DuBois now?" I asked.

"He became a bankrupt and fled the colony, leaving his estate to his creditors. Mrs. DuBois is here with us—in hiding—with Joanna to attend her. I expect at some time she will fly from here."

I looked out of the window, and there in the garden was lovely Joanna, cutting flowers for the household.

43

She was taller than middle size and elegantly shaped. She moved her well-formed limbs with more than common gracefulness. Her face was full of the modesty of her people, and her black eyes were large and full of expression. In spite of her dark skin, her cheeks showed a vermilion tinge. Her nose was well formed and small, and when she spoke she showed two rows of regular and wonderfully white teeth. Her hair was dark brown with lighter streaks and formed a crest of ringlets in which she had worked flowers and gold spangles. Round her neck, her arms, and her ankles she wore gold chains, rings, amulets, and medals, all presents from her father before his death.

A shawl of Indian muslin thrown around her polished shoulders partially covered her bosom. A petticoat of rich chintz completed her apparel and acted as a mirror for her shapely hips. Slave girl or not, she was a distinguished and beguiling young girl who was beautiful by even the most stringent standards.

I watched her with increasing desire and decided to be her friend and to protect her as far as I could, for to agitate such a fine body with the whip, hot iron rods, or any other instrument of torture would be sacrilegious.

The rains had not ceased, and this compelled the rebel Africans to keep to their settlements. The mosquitoes, however, were so plentiful that I was unable to sleep, and I grew so fretful I became sick. Each day my house was crowded with visitors. At last Mr. Kennedy allowed me a boy of about twelve called Quaco to stay with me and carry my umbrella. He sat outside the door and informed all callers that "Massera he sleep—dead-sleep."

44

All the while I thought of no one but Joanna, and she became a torture to my heart. And then one day she came with her sister Beatrice, a girl I had seen before, to visit me and breakfast with me.

Joanna, I discovered, had been well educated by her father, but since his death she had not given much time to her schooling. She read fluently in Dutch and German and spoke heavily accented English as well as Surinam creole. For fear of being accused of forgetting her station, she was careful to conceal her accomplishments. She hardly ever spoke and kept quietly to herself.

"When I am at Fauconberg locked in my room, I am as good as all those who would beat me and call me a slave," she said.

My heart shuddered at the thought of what could overtake her at any time. A misunderstood gesture, a hasty word, a broken plate, any of these "mistakes" could cause her to be mutilated or killed. I took her in my arms and felt her shudder.

"What do you want of me, my friend, my master?" she asked with a look that tortured and amused me at the same time.

"To love you, Joanna. Deeply. Truly. In your presence my feelings become sublime and I believe in virtue and commitment and even in the existence of angels. I want to purchase you, educate you, and keep you always with me."

Her laughter was like the sound of beautifully tuned bells. And then in a flash she looked bewildered and terrified of an unseen keeper.

"Captain Stedman," she said, "I am born a low, contemptible slave. Were you to treat me with too much attention, you must disgrace yourself with all your friends and relations, while the purchase of my freedom you will find expensive, difficult, and impossible. Though only a slave, I have a soul, I hope not inferior to any European. You have distinguished me as much above all others of my unhappy birth. You have, sir, pitied me, and now, independent of every thought, I shall have pride in throwing myself at your feet till fate shall part us or you find other reasons to banish me from your presence."

"Oh, dear Joanna. How can I persuade you to believe in my sincerity? You do not have to be my slave—simply my lover, my wife!"

"Captain, sir, your love has been mislaid. Do you know what I must do? I must live wearing yet another coat of deception—educated but uneducated, your wife but yet a slave girl who must be hired from the owners of Fauconberg, who wears the given dress of a woman of mixed race sometimes and a lady's dress when we are alone. I must never forget that I am a slave. And will you mind when your drunken friends accost and command me? Lolkens, De Graav, Kennedy?"

"I will inform them of my intention to marry you. And I can assure you they are honorable men."

She laughed again. "Yes," she said, "when they are sober. Why did you send me all those presents with Quaco? I do not need them."

All night I paced the room while Quaco shouted, "Massera, sleepy, sleepy!"

Finally I did fall asleep, and I found when I awoke late in the day that Joanna had visited and had returned all the money I had spent on presents for her. She had, by taking back the goods personally to the vendors, persuaded them to refund my cash. Beside the money was a note explaining that by rights even my presents belonged to her master.

Her honesty had not only charm but a comprehensiveness about it which pleased me and indeed made me realize just how deeply in love I was. For the first time I wanted to be tethered to a wife, a home, and perhaps a family, with a woman who was both lovely and virtuous.

I discussed my intention to purchase and educate Joanna with my friends. But even the best of them remonstrated with me. "Are you mad?" they said. "Keep your sighs in your belly and do what we do!"

"And what of the children you beget?" I asked.

"What of them? They go, according to slave custom, with their mothers, as calves go with cows and foals with mares. What do we care? Nature is like a great show resembling an opera!"

Deflowering and cohabiting with slave girls—especially the beautiful ones—was a kind of sport that even the most conservative and goodly men found themselves engaged in. The pressure to participate in this sport was considerable, since the quarry was captive and on pain of death could not refuse. When I thought of sweet Joanna being ravished or beaten, brutalized or tortured, a burning panic seized me.

None could dissuade me from protecting Joanna. The more I knew her, the more obvious to me her bewilderment and her fears became. A part of her appeared dead. I refer to that part of her mind that would query situations, examine them, and either agree with or object to them. I thought of all those women I had known whose chances to express themselves were so pitiful because of their brutal lives. Childbirth alone, with crude surgical implements, was a constant source of fear, and every other independence was denied them. I would not let Joanna waste her intelligence and her imagination. She was a slave, but I was determined to keep my wedding as I would have done in Scotland, although it was necessary only to declare in the presence of a witness that it was our desire to become man and wife in wedlock.

As I thought once more of my sweet love, a verse of John Donne's poem just as beautiful as she was came to my lips.

"I wonder by my troth, what thou, and I
Did, till we lov'd? Were we not wean'd till then
But suck'd on country pleasures, childishly
Or snorted we in the seven sleepers' den?
It was so; but this, all pleasures' fancies be
If ever any beauty did I see,
Which I desir'd, and got, 'twas but a dream of thee,
And now good morrow to our waking souls
Which watch not one another out of fear,
For love, all love of other sight controls,
And makes one little room, an everywhere."

I was not aware that I had been overheard reciting this verse by the slave girl Claudia and her mistress. "Splendid, sir," said Mrs. Demelly. "My husband never wooed me so! You must keep the wedding in my home. I do so love weddings! If I could but will it, Joshua and I could have one such every month, to remind him how much I regret my leisure and my dependence upon him."

I looked at her—this pretty, dark-haired woman, rendered more divine by her expensive clothes and her easy, superior manner.

Her husband now entered and paid his compliments. He then congratulated me on my conquest and informed me, "She is a serious girl. Her father made her too high-quality. He forgot her station, and the thought of what her fate might be killed him."

Later Lolkens, too, congratulated me. "Whatever I can do to help protect her I'll do," he promised.

I gave Joanna the medal my father had given to my mother on the night I was born, but such was her modesty that she wore it round her neck and asked me never to mention it in the presence of my friends. The following day, in a show of sincere gratitude for their kind indulgences, she of her own will thanked the Demellys by curtsying deeply before them. And then once more to Mr. and Mrs. Lolkens, which made them feel uplifted, although but one word could adequately describe them—rich.

That night Joanna's mother, Cery, and her sister Lucretia came to tell me what they thought of my intentions of taking Joanna among the white people as if she were one of them. Cery was quite a young woman—about seven or eight years to her fortieth year—as slave girls were taken to bed at around ten or eleven years of age.

"I came to speak my mind, Cap'n Stedman," Cery said. "Joanna is a slave, but slaves have family. All our family live at Fauconberg, and we have to keep a wedding there to satisfy my father's heart. He is old and blind, and he must not grieve. Joanna did not just come from smoke."

Lucretia, Cery's pretty younger sister, said nothing, but when I agreed to their suggestion she placed a box of delicious-looking biscuits on the table. Lucretia was famous for her delicious biscuits.

Another woman waited outside. "That is Quaco's mama," Cery said. "Not real mama, but somebody must take in children who have no family. We black slaves mother all children who slavery robs of parents."

Quaco had told me of his history, and it had brought sorrow to my heart. His parents had been farmers and had lived by hunting and fishing and wandering on the coast shore, where for one brief moment they had left Quaco and his brothers. But in that instant child stealers seized them and, placing them in a sack, sold them along with several hundred more to the King of Guinea. They worked from dawn to dusk. Then one day the King suddenly died; all his slaves were to be beheaded at his funeral. Quaco with a lust for life hid in a field of corn. Later he was found by a captain in the King's army. He promised to keep Quaco, but instead he sold the boy to a Dutch slaver for a musket and gunpowder. When Quaco was brought to Surinam, afraid and forlorn, Mrs. Kennedy bought him. It was there, I suppose, that the woman known as Ma Dede took him to her heart.

On this night, with a moon so full of light and wonder, the shadows so deep, the wind and sea a harmony of sound, I felt happiness, tangible and all-embracing, for the first time in my life. I had heard of this feeling, but now I knew it, for merely thinking of Joanna released such joy in me I was certain I could die of it. I readily agreed to meet all her family at Fauconberg Plantation the following evening.

I dressed with great care and must have looked an imposing sight, judging by the sounds of wonder with which the reception committee greeted me. In my deepest soul I knew I was to declare love for my true love.

The music from the native instruments was subdued but not unpleasant.

50

Quaco carried the presents in a large basket on his head. Being musically inclined, I was keen to look at the instruments. With Joanna breathtaking in an elaborate dress of pure white silk, a wreath of flowers in her hair, we presented a bottle of rum, some tobacco, and some biscuits to the players. The instruments—such as the *kimba toto,* the *ansoko bina,* the *papa* drum, the *qua-qua,* the *corema,* the *benta,* the *too-too* or flute, and the trumpet—were all homemade.

Quaco walked behind me, still with the basket of presents on his head. I thought I would be alone on this auspicious night, but several of the well-married men had brought beautiful concubines along to be part of the wonderful ceremony of these, in essence, cultured people.

Joanna's grandfather, his white hair like a thick cap upon his head, blessed us. After touching me (since he was blind), he accepted my presents of money, tobacco, and sweets. I wished he could have seen my Joanna in that simple white silk gown, the circlet of orange blossoms in her hair. She was such a beautiful girl that at the sight of her that night I thought of nature as a splendid artist who had constructed her most painstakingly, with every regard to proportion.

We sat together to receive congratulations and to distribute small gifts. When it was over, Joanna disappeared among the women. It was now Cery's turn.

"You have to 'know' Joanna, and if you don't, you have to pay me. A man must know his woman," she said curtly.

They brought before me a woman draped from head to foot in a sheet.

"That is Joanna?" Cery asked expectantly.

"No," I said. "Too short."

A huge wave of laughter poured over the room. I offered Cery a present of a headkerchief like those she wore. They now brought out another person. I could clearly see that it was Joanna's plump sister Beatrice, who was well on the way to being a little barrel.

"No," I said again. "Too plump. Not Joanna."

Cery held out her hand again.

Finally they brought out the stately Joanna. I pulled off the sheet and called out, "Here she is. Joanna!"

Cery then questioned us about how we intended to live together in harmony and then counseled us in the ways of a good wife and a good husband.

Everyone was jubilant. The music and feasting started, but Joanna and I walked alone outside.

"Where is Lolkens?" I asked.

She shrugged. "Exercising his ownership rights somewhere."

"And the overseer?"

"Asleep somewhere also. This is a big plantation! Women are many and have no choice."

I felt part of the woods and the rivers and the mountains in the distance. Part of being beyond the earth, part of the cosmic forces and the design of creation. In the most unexpected way I had found myself grounded, and this ritual was part of it. I kissed my bride—such a kiss. I was full to bursting with love for her.

I felt cleansed of all the evils that, as a European, my race had initiated. I had experienced a warmth that was boundless in its expression. And I thanked God for the opportunity to know Joanna's people and be a part of their family. There were no myths left to explore. They danced; they sang, laughed, and cried. And were often beaten to death.

The next afternoon I visited Mr. Demelly, who, with his lady, congratulated me on my "recovery from sickness." One of the ladies in the company assured me that while my marriage was perhaps censured by some, it was applauded by many and, she believed in her heart, envied by all. They held a "decent wedding" for us, at which many of our respectable friends made their appearances and at which I was as happy as any bridegroom ever was. I concluded the ceremony of my marriage to my utmost satisfaction. I could have taken Joanna, commanded her, but she would not have me on those terms. I wanted her love, but I wanted her to give it willingly to me, and I took the just route to obtain it. She explained much to me. The planters had town houses in Paramaribo and Surinam and plantations along the Surinam River. But wherever slaves may go they must always return to the plantation at which they were *owned*.

Three

I had foolishly assumed that I could live at peace in my home with my wife and our servants, one black, one white, but the laws of the land did not allow it. Joanna had to be at the beck and call of the Fauconberg plantation and could visit me to sleep only when time allowed. On those days when it was impossible for her to come to me, I visited; it was a situation that proved grossly wrong. When we were apart, I imagined her in dire situations, manacled and calling for help that I could not offer her. To free her, I would have to purchase her, and the laws of the land put every difficulty in the ways of those who chose that path.

Upon returning from Fauconberg one day, I heard of the death of young Lieutenant Lantmann after an attack of a fever, and I was sorely grieved that this young man whom I liked so well, by the neglect of both our physician and our colonel had been allowed to die. I attended the funeral at Fort Zeelandia and stood beside his grave thinking of him as I had once known him—so polite and eager to do his duty—when I was disturbed by frenetic laughter and other diabolical sounds. Imagine my surprise—nay, my shock—to see the captured rebel Africans gleefully clanking their chains by which they were fettered as they trundled around to supervise the roasting of yams and potatoes on the sepulchers of those brave Europeans who had been sacrificed in the struggle against them.

"Build your fires elsewhere!" I ordered. "These men have died in the cause!"

One, obviously a leader, laughed, to reveal large slabs of teeth, and said, "Dey deade. Dey no feel! Dey same as slaves!"

I returned to my house full of anger, but his remark made me think. As I passed the courthouse a crowd had gathered where two men, one white, the other African, were being punished for stealing. I argued loudly that the African, being a child of nature, had followed instructions. He should not lose his life while the white man was mildly beaten and sent on his way, only to be sympathized with and brought back later.

I felt a hand upon my shoulder; the hand was that of a respectably clad young man. He said, "Sir, from your remarks I gather that you are but newly arrived. The other day, sir, I saw with my own eyes an African suspended alive from the gallows by the ribs, between which an incision had been made to accommodate the hook. He hung alive for three whole days, sipping only the water that ran down his face from the merciful rain, which alone saved him from dire thirst and from the taunts of passersby who loathed the wet weather. He never groaned or shed a tear, but said that no evil of the European was strong enough to make him weep.

"There are many like him. You may roast them alive, break them upon the rack, lacerate and salt them, expose them to plagues and torments of insects, but they would not weep or moan to satisfy your expectations or cause you to cease your actions. They bear suffering as Christ bore his, only the Heavenly Father is unknown to them."

Had it not been said that black skin prevented the true development of feeling? The man's words had indeed made a notch upon my everyday thinking, and with the passing of time I found his words wholly true. The punishment of slaves was extreme because it was thought they felt less pain.

We had been sent to fight the rebels of Surinam, but due to the long wet season they had gone to ground inside their settlements. The soldiers, thick and idle about the streets, aroused the anger of the colonists, who called upon the troops to go home, having become too great an expense upon the public purse. But fate took a hand. News came that the Patamaca rebels who lived in the dense jungle around the river had been on the move and had ambushed Captain Lepper and his party of men.

The rebels had, it appeared, captured a European child. Having had warning of the approach of Lepper's party, the rebels caused the child to cry, its voice being familiar to white men. Then they allowed a glimpse of the child. The soldiers, not knowing that the approach to the settlement led to a quagmire, sank up to their shoulders in this grave from which there was no escape. The rebels pulled them out one by one, the executioner shouting at them in triumph, "We go killie you! Daggo. Wha' for you come?"

He shot them one by one as they struggled out of the mud. They were then stripped of their clothes, their hands taken as trophies, and their heads left to mark the spot where they had been murdered.

The news caused a tumult in the town. The rebels were led by a relentless fighter called Zam-Zam from the colony of Berbice, who had tried to start a settlement on the river. But the jungle was not dense enough, and the Indians betrayed him to soldiers, who cut his family to pieces.

Fourgeoud was lampooned, but made no attempt to hunt down the rebels until two trackers, Okera and Gowasary, arrived to join his party as private soldiers. They were men of darkness who, before being pardoned for delivering their Chief Atta to the governor of Berbice, had committed atrocities against Europeans. Now firm favorites with the colonel, they behaved so badly to my men I was forced to tell them both that if they did not behave better, feathers would by nightfall grow from the ends of their noses. After that they sat as if entranced. Out of the corner of my eye I could see them touching their noses to see if the feathers had indeed sprouted.

At Cometibo the rebels struck again, and this time we were given our orders to follow them into the jungle and destroy their settlements. Joanna had been expecting this separation, but when it came she was thrown into a state of deepest worry. There would be miles of river between us, and what if she were to be given orders to be of service to visitors to Fauconberg? We discussed this. She did not reply but opening one of the medals she wore, showed me that it contained a herb that can put to rest too ardent lovers or send them quietly to sleep.

"Parents cannot control our ends, but we are all taught how to take care of ourselves—only we must never be found out. Do you think we like what happens to us?" she said to me.

I kissed her again and again, wishing that I could take her with me. I bid her take care of our home and sent one of my men to convey the baggage at her direction. Tears trembled in her eyes and my heart ached for love of her, but duty bound me as truly as that love between us.

My detail was to patrol the upper regions of the Cottica and Patamaca rivers, tributaries of the river Surinam, with twenty-five men besides my boy Quaco, all in high spirits at the prospect of a close encounter with the rebels. Up the river, the landscape looked dense and green after the rains. Monkeys of all sorts were at play in the trees, but not a sign of the rebels did we see. I noticed a toucan or banana beak—a most colorful bird, the bill as sizable as its body—as it watched us from a leafy tree.

Camaraca, one of the African soldiers, said, "Massera, see dat bird! He banana beak. He talk too much. He see Watra Mama come out of the river and sit down. He say Watra Mama she got no foot! She got tail like fish! Watra Mama she got no foot! He tell everybody. Then he get thirsty. When he go to drink, Watra Mama hold his beak to pull him in and drownded him. But he fly and he beak it swell and it stay so big. Dat bird he tell Watra Mama secret."

I knew by this that Camaraca was a member of the Winti cult, which venerated the God of the Sea. Camaraca knew stories about every bird, about flowers, about everything, even about the mosquitoes that gleefully devoured us each night.

We stopped at Barbacoeba. The residents had seen nothing of the rebels, but offered us provisions and warned us of the climate, which they were sure would kill us. I felt so refreshed after that short stop that I would do naught but need my Joanna. Thoughts of her were like an ache—sometimes dull and distant, sometimes so strong I could feel her presence. The Africans built me a hut at this place which was called Hope and stood at the mouth of the creek Comewina.

That night I wrote to Joanna:

My True Love,

I am sure that sometimes you are here with me, although I cannot see you. Are you putting your time to good use? If you feel lonely, ask a visit with Zubbly Sampson, a mulatto also married to a white man. I have written asking her to befriend you. Did you know her husband was an Englishman who took her to England, where I will take you some day?

I have seen and drawn pretty flowers and many strange animals. Tomorrow I will walk barefoot at Brockstyne Plantation, which Camaraca says will be good for me. The chigoes* will have their way with my toes.

I will be on this river for three months, and three weeks are already gone. Remember, my sweet love, that you are always in my heart. Have you received the baskets I made for you and sent last week? I have learned to make them with Quaco to help me.

I remain your true love.

John

We rowed down the Casepeore. So very thick were the mosquitoes now that by clapping my hands I killed several dozen. Following Camaraca's advice, I swam twice daily, always keeping my limbs in motion to fool the alligators stealthily lurking underwater, as well as the *perai* or piranha, those bloodthirsty fish. I shed my soldier's uniform and my shoes, preferring to go barefoot and dressed in a cotton shirt and trousers. We learned that the enemy had been seen hovering around the *Cerberus* as she had been moored in a shallow part of the river.

Our patrol found nothing, but on our way back a feeble voice hailed us from a little clearing in the forest.

---

*Fleas that live in the fleshy parts of the feet.

I decided to investigate. An old, decrepit woman, destitute in a hut no larger than a dog kennel, lived there with her cats. Europeans had killed her husband, and her Jewish master had abandoned her there to support his right of possession of the land. She had only a few plantain trees, yams, and cassava and nothing more. Beside her was an effigy of her husband, which she talked to and kept for company. I gave her some barley, salt beef, and a bottle of rum, for which she offered me a cat, which I refused.

We passed the Devil's Harwar, a campsite for the military and one of the unhealthiest places in the world. It was the harbor of every insect that was a plague upon this earth. We found a dry spot after crawling over marshes overgrown with underwood and came to a rebel village. There was no one about except the skeleton of a man who had been tied to a tree and left to die of insects and exposure.

I felt feverish as I lay in my hammock in the boat. The sentinel called to me, saying that he'd seen a man moving in the brushwood on the beach. I immediately dropped anchor and, with a small party, stepped ashore to reconnoiter.

"Massera," said David, an African soldier, "dis be not man. Dis be snakee."

We decided to follow, David cutting a path with his bill hook. We had not gone more than twenty yards when the lad, almost rigid with concentration, called out, "Me see snakee!"

There lay the huge animal, rolled up under the rubble, flicking its tongue, its eyes bright as fire. I aimed, fired, and missed its head. It flounced around in its niche, showering us with muddy water. I fired again; this time it was subdued but not dead. We brought the boat rope and, making a noose, put it over the snake's head and allowed it to swim with us to the settlement at Barbacoeba.

David climbed a tree with an end of the rope and suspended the snake from the branches. Then, a knife between his teeth, he clung with arms and legs around the monster, incising and stripping the skin and at the same time bathing in the blood of the snake. The snakeskin was wide enough to encircle twelve-year-old Quaco. The Africans ate the flesh heartily, and the creature gave us four gallons of fat, which was greatly prized as a cure for burns and bruises and for which the surgeons at Devil's Harwar thanked us.

I wrote once more to Joanna.

My True Love,

Had you not been at the end of my journey home, I would have abandoned myself to the pests that occupy every corner of this place. I shot a *sarcawinkee,* a little monkey that I have drawn. It was really good eating! The Africans caught a sloth but left its legs behind on the tree, which it had grasped so firmly they had to cut the animal free.

Two of my officers are in hospital. We are running short of supplies, but our colonel seems to think that poor food strengthens men. I have begun to feel that no one loves me but you, Joanna. In the loneliness of the darkness the stars twinkle at me and I remember your smile. You are always here in the sounds and colors of nature and in the beams of sunlight that chance to wander through the foliage.

I send you my heart.

Your True Love,
John

The mail arrived, with letters from Mama, Captain Stoeleman, Kennedy, and Mrs. Godefrooy, a wealthy widow and benefactress who also sent me stores of rum, meat, bread, and claret. I knew her well, having visited at her beautiful plantation Alkmar, where she treated me as one of her own. I had not heard from Joanna and was consumed with anxiety about her fate, which could be changed so rapidly for the worst at the whim of a delinquent overseer who had gone crazy with power.

While I brooded, orders came from Fourgeoud to pursue the rebels who had burned down three plantations. He completely ignored the fact that his men were dying of the life in the bush, where we were exposed to ringworm, looseness, and bellyjack and to creatures such as bloodsucking bats that twice bled my toe as well as rats, spiders, bush worms, ants, ticks, wood lice, and scorpions.

We could not ignore the growling jaguars or the constantly jabbering monkeys overhead or the alligators and *perai* eagerly waiting to strip flesh from bones in the rivers. The deadly plants, like the *mocco-mocco,* the juice from which caused itching almost to madness, the baboon-knife or razor grass that cut like cutlasses, leeches that lived in swamps and could overpower a man in minutes, all these things waited for us at every turn. Added to everything was the weather; hot, dry savannas that combusted at will; icy cold nights; boiling sun and heavy rains. When sick we were served by a callous, indifferent physician and an absent, gossiping colonel who showed open favoritism to undeserving men and who did not balk at insulting his officers in front of them whenever the opportunity presented itself.

Colonel Fourgeoud wrote commiserating with me and sent me some relief troops, but the men continued to die. And then, praise be to the Almighty, a barge arrived from Paramaribo with the proper reinforcements, ammunition, provisions, and medicines and a different surgeon to tend us.

My own health was on the point of collapse, but, with a group of men who had suffered indescribably, I returned to Devil's Harwar to find a quantity of commodities from my sweet Joanna. There was a letter from Stoeleman, a captain like myself who had been tracking the rebels. There was also one from Joanna that gladdened my heart.

Dear Captain,

I wish I had words in my head to put side by side with those you send to me. I have not and so I must love you by doing all you tell me to do. My eyes will look with all good blessing on your drawings.

I hope you got all the eggs and fruit I have sent. The days are long for me, and I wish you would come back. La Marre has taken Beatrice to his plantation. He has already more than twenty children. One of them, Jettee, has gone to school in Holland. In the middle of all the noise of Fauconberg, I am lonely for you.

My best wishes to you.

Joanna

I was delighted with all her news. She feared that Fourgeoud would open my mail and so was very circumspect in her letters, but whenever she wrote my heart soared and I was extremely indulgent to Quaco and the men.

The next day I woke up with a fever, and by the middle of the day I was in an extremely confounded state. I read Stoeleman's letter again:

63

Sir,

This is to acquaint you that the rebels have burned three estates by your side—Suyingheyd, Peru, and L'Esperance—the ruins of which I heard are still smoking—and that they have cut the throats of all white inhabitants who fell in their way. As on their retreat they must pass close by where you are posted, be on your guard. I am in haste.

Yours etc.,
Stoeleman

Somehow the news of the rebel attack preceded my announcement to the troops in the hospital at Devil's Harwar. The men, sick, maimed or dying, burst out of their hammocks, rushing, overthrowing themselves, scrabbling, crawling on all fours, bandages unraveled and entangled in hurrying feet. Never had I beheld such a commotion in the preservation of a miserable life—men quivering for fear of death at the hands of those whose lives they had liberally taken. They made for the farthest corners of the boats and the bush, not realizing that their moans and shrieking alone would betray them to the rebels, should they come.

Fear stalked the community with steps as tangible as those of a sentinel on guard. Never was darkness more abhorred and the daylight more welcomed. The paths were strewn with dead, whom we buried in their hammocks. It had all been a false alarm, there had been no fire, no smoking ruins, and no rebels passed even close to us, but the men continued to die of shock day by day and one by one.

I had got so sick I gave myself leave to go to Paramaribo. All night the fever kept hold of my system. My body ached and itched. As we passed De Marre's plantation, a light showed.

I sent an African to ask a lantern, but De Marre himself came out. Upon catching sight of me he called for Joanna's sister Beatrice to prepare a bed for me.

"You must rest here tonight, Stedman," he said. "Please accept my hospitality. You must not do your constitution further harm." Such a kindly man he was, I accepted.

They took me indoors and placed me upon crisp, clean sheets, fed me appropriately, and sent for my sweet Joanna. She arrived with a physician, who bled me and applied cures to my ringworm and to the two sores, the work of leeches, on my thigh.

I noticed a bruise on Joanna's face, and after much persuasion, she informed me that a soldier had accosted her and struck her because she did not obey his demands.

"What did he do?" I asked.

"He dragged me off to your house, where I offered him a drink. Soon after he complained of *belly-hatty** and left. He was not well at all from the moment he had his drink."

"Where is he?"

"I know not. He was taken away. He was so drunk, you see." She spoke calmly but with determination that her dignity would be hers until she died. I questioned her more, but she never revealed how she and her sisters kept themselves for the men of their choice.

"We found an old woman in the woods," I said. "She came to ask us to celebrate the day of her husband's death five years ago, when he killed an overseer who had ill-treated her for spurning his attentions. She threw food

---

*Dry dysentery.

upon the river and, with a basket of fruit and flowers, visited all the places where they used to sit."

"That is the custom. Sometimes people take little effigies," Joanna replied. "We believe that life goes on. When my grandfather dies, the first born after that day would be him reborn."

"I felt sad for this poor woman all alone," I said.

"Silence has voices of its own. But your people cannot hear them. They do not know how to read the silences. She was not alone. Her man was with her, as you would always be with me."

I held her close, transporting to her all my elemental need of her. "Joanna," I said. "Oh, Joanna. I do bless the day you came into my life."

She picked up a picture of four wild orchids I had drawn.

"Each one means something—a wish, a dream, laughter, and love," I said. "They are yours."

She gave me a look. Oh, such a look. It spoke ten thousand words.

It was October now, and I was ready to proceed upon my second campaign. Instead of a tent boat to afford protection from the sun, I found a greasy yawl with a few drunken Dutch sailors waiting for me. This was one of Fourgeoud's ways of insulting me. He seemed to get a callous pleasure out of resenting my actions and to start subterranean fires and then put them out again. I refused to enter the yawl and began to rail against the injustice. I was supported in my complaint by some English and Americans who were bent on tweaking Dutch noses, and of course a fight broke out, with wigs, hats, and bottles flying. A mob collected, each taking one side or the other, and the fighting continued until ten o'clock that night. I was exhausted and slept well into the next day. At six o'clock I said good-bye to dear Joanna, hoisted my colors, and departed up the river in an English tent boat that had been supplied at my colonel's extraordinary intervention as a peace maker. He was a treacherous man!

We rowed to the three estates and at L'Esperance, where I was later to build a beautiful and spacious house for my family, I met a soldier who had miraculously escaped from the rebels.

"How did you accomplish that feat?" I asked. "The devils give no quarter."

"A miracle, sir! Before God, a miracle!" he replied. "They had surrounded the large dwelling house of the absent planter and were most meticulously setting fire to it. I fled to the garret and prayed that they would disperse, but I was disappointed. The flames rose higher and higher. I could feel the heat rushing toward me. 'Merciful God,' I prayed, 'save me! I hate no man. Dear God, save my life.'

"With those words I jumped into the midst of my sorely surprised enemies, landed upon my feet, and plunged into the river. They came after me, hunting me like an animal with sabers, cutlasses, and bill hooks. Unable to swim, I clung to the *mocco-mocco* plants while holding my breath. I felt as if my heart would burst, but they, assuming me to be drowned, departed. I climbed out and sat upon the grass until I was taken up from my predicament by your boat."

I gave the poor creature a glass of rum, and the night being come upon us, we all lay down to sleep. The next day I woke early. The men having caught an armadillo, I set about drawing it and afterward swam, paddled, and watched the sport of animals in the jungle, all against the arrival of Colonel Fourgeoud.

He came shortly after, and we proceeded to attack the enemy in the Rice Country, named thus because they had grown rice in great proportions. That was at Boosy Cray, Bonny's country. Bonny was an inveterate hater of Europeans, whom he did not hesitate to flog to death and treat in the same manner as blacks were treated, for the entertainment of his people.

We met some soldiers whom another rebel leader had set upon the path to safety. "You daggo," he had told them. "Go find your massa and tell him that Bonny no dead! Bonny great man! Gado sa bresse Bonny! [God bless Bonny]."

We brought the men into our boat, fed them, and sent them down the river.

Colonel Fourgeoud had proved himself ungentlemanly by discussing my trousers, which he called skirt-petticoats, to amuse his favorites. I confronted him, but he was not easily brought to book. Instead, he read out some articles of conduct that should be observed in the woods:

1. Quietness and sobriety are strongly recommended.
2. On pain of death, never fire without order.
3. Death for losing arms or for plundering while engaging the enemy.
4. An officer or sergeant is to inspect distribution of the victuals at all times.
5. Each officer is to be limited in the number of Africans attending him.

It was a useless exercise, as all the rules were well known to the men. I could see from Fourgeoud's manner that there was mischief afoot, and by commanding his troops, sick or well, to march out in search of the enemy he murdered many of them. He returned with three rebels who had been surprised when seeking food; one managed to escape, but another, with his leg shot to slivers, was bound hand and foot to a pole like a dead hog. He moaned in his pain and misery and, mercifully, died that night.

The next week we marched for three days in good weather to the Wana Creek. I was so tired I fell into an exhausted sleep.

Some hours later the sentinel shook me awake and I heard Fourgeoud swearing loudly and accusing me of speaking. I denied. He continued his swearing, and to hear those vile words proceeding from underneath his aging mustache moved me to laughter. My laughter was so immoderate it was taken up by the men and, subsequently, by Fourgeoud himself.

The next day he set a captive African named September, the month of his birth, at liberty; September followed us in a dogged, good-natured way. On we marched, the heat growing more intolerable with every step. We searched for water, but none could we find. The men rose early and, crawling on all fours, licked water from the leaves. Fourgeoud, in spite of these hardships, insisted we move forward and fed the troops salt beef. The men's thirst became intolerable. Suddenly Fourgeoud fell facedown upon the earth, his lips and tongue parched black.

They marveled at my stamina. But it was no stamina; it was the work of Quaco, who secured for me each morning water from the wild pineapple plants. That day I could not drink without first offering some to my colonel, so old and gone he looked. Revived, he sent the tracker Gowasary to find water. Quaco took a bottle and headed for the pit we had secretly dug. He managed to fill the bottle with water, but on his return he encountered the colonel, who demanded to know what it contained.

"Water, Massera," replied Quaco.

Like a spoiled child, Fourgeoud smashed the bottle to pieces with the butt of his gun. By now all the men had found the pit and, plunging into it, quickly reduced it to a mire.

We slung our hammocks in an old rebel camp, and I lay fulminating against the colonel for his childish ways. But more was to come. An African soldier who was sick asked for a glass of wine, and out of my own store I gave it to him. The colonel forbade it and, seizing the wine returned it to the bottle, saying, "Drink it yourself or give none."

I controlled my anger by looking at the moon high up outside. I walked around, enjoying the scenery and thinking of the girl I loved and, quite accidentally found water. I rushed back shouting, "Water! Water!"

Everyone rushed out. The taste was sweet and all drank heartily. Afterward Fourgeoud ordered his supper to be boiled.

"And what must become of ours?" I asked.

"Eat it raw," he replied. "Raw beef and raw pork."

I waited my time and dropped my piece into his pot. Later Quaco fetched it for me, much to the amusement of the men.

I wrote to Joanna, telling her that all was well and that I had drawn many rare and strange birds. It began to rain, and with the rains came the flies and the mosquitoes.

Captain Federicy, who had taken out a party of men, to our joy returned with a captive African in chains. He was called Cupido, but in spite of torture in the extreme he refused to betray his companions. Disheartened, we felt that our sufferings had yielded nothing. Then a rebel and his wife came to us of their own free will and surrendered. They had been starving in the woods, for they looked like scarecrows. They groveled at Fourgeoud's feet and showed their teeth in submission. He picked up his blunderbuss and aimed at them. They did not cry, but the man bared his chest and the woman turned her back. They waited for the bang, but it never came. He sat them down and fed them.

We set course for Paramaribo and before long were among friends. I sent for my inestimable wife, and she cried both from joy at my survival and regret at my pitiable condition. It was impossible to be a husband and lover to her, so weak was I. But my affection for her increased as each day I sampled her devotion. She returned to Fauconberg and I to my house to recover my strength, but each day she came to tend me with affection and care.

And then suddenly she did not come! I stayed in bed for two days, annoyed that there had been no sign of my wife. And then Fate drew me out into the street to see the selling of slaves and plantations.

Imagine my surprise when I discovered that Fauconberg, with all its stock of buildings and slaves, was to be sold. There they all were, the sleepy, white-haired old man, Beatrice, Cery, Cojo, Joanna, Henry, all of them—my family who loved me so well. I was at once thrown into a state of great distress and began to imagine the countless miseries that could befall them. What could I do? I rushed around, asking how I could stop the selling of Joanna, but I could not. Mercifully, my friend Lolkens was appointed administrator of the estate, and he brought Joanna to me. Weeping, I held her to my heart almost unable to think how close to losing her I had come.

"Anything I can do to be of service to you, Stedman," Lolkens said, "you need only say."

I thanked him with only relief and gratitude in my heart.

"Do you see?" Joanna sobbed. "You will never be able to protect me. It was the same with my parents. My father loved us so much, but nothing he did could save us and he died trying."

They were all resigned to their fate, without will and without hope. I tried to imagine what thoughts went through the minds of parents, grandparents, husbands, wives, and children.

I took Joanna in my arms. What could I do to assure her of my love? She was so silent it was as if something had died in her supple, sweet-smelling body. I made explosive love to her, but the terror of being sold had killed her desire for me. Hope had died within her, and slavery had killed it.

The next day I dined with Mrs. Demelly, and we spoke of the terror that was slavery.

"Our women could never imagine it," I said. "They see the beads of sweat upon their slaves' faces and the shine upon their sable skins and say, 'How wonderful!' But it is fear, searing fear, that makes them sweat and shine."

"Oh, fie, sir," she replied. "We have our terrors, too. I know of a young lady who in her youth fell in love with an Apollo of a slave—a quadroon called Justin. He avoided. She pursued. He hid, knowing she was forbidden, but she cornered him and gave him every instruction. And then one day when she had confined him in her lust, who should appear but her father on horseback. Prepared for all emergencies, she shot the beautiful Justin and accused him of the crime of rape. Though dead, he was broken upon the rack, and she lives with this guilt, concealing it in good works and kind deeds."

"Madam, I beg pardon. I spoke too rashly."

"We are not saints, sir, though our husbands make us out to be. I admire your love of Joanna and your commitment, and I hope that God will bless your love in many ways."

I thanked her for her friendship. She had never once failed me, but always behaved unselfishly in my interests.

The night was quite lively when I walked home, but I felt dark in heart and mind. The wounds from the injustices of slavery were bleeding into the most distant corners of my life. I was conscious of the fact that I straddled two worlds—one a castle I entered by race alone, and the other a castle entered by love alone. Sometimes both failed my expectations. Often I watched as some masters tried to drown their slaves in oppression. Too well I recall Marquis who had a wife and two small children whom he loved; he labored hard generally and finished his task of digging his trench of five hundred feet by four o'clock in the afternoon so that he could tend his small garden and provide vegetables for his beloved family. Along came his *humane* master, who had been apprised of his industry. "If you dig five hundred feet by four o'clock, you must work till sunset and dig six hundred feet!" he said. The poor young man was condemned to toil for a full two hours more. He could not escape. He watched his children die of pellagra from the lack of fresh vegetables.

Four

I had rented a house in Surinam for use when I came out of the woods. I was at home for no more than a half hour when Van Halm and Francen, two gaming friends, dropped by. We exchanged greetings. Seeing me so low, they attempted to elevate my spirits by presenting some bottles of claret, which we proceeded to drink without further hesitation. We dined on ham and bread, the last of my store, and later in the evening, staggering like sailors who had emptied an alehouse, we were rowed to Plantation Sporkesgift, a beautiful place Van Halm had inherited from his father. The slaves fawned around him, but later turned their attention to us. In keeping with tradition, we effectively scrutinized them as one would whatever could be had for the taking, and chose the best.

I made a perplexing choice of a petite quadroon called Cecily. Silent and young though she was, she did not conceal her distaste for her position and her contempt for the service she was expected to render. She was around seventeen years old, and there seemed to be an inner agony that left a stain in her dark-blue, nearsighted eyes; she wore a scowl that with goodwill might have served as a smile. She slept with me upon the bed, but on my pretending to snore she leapt from beside me and lay upon the floor, weeping softly. She was perhaps thinking of the beating she would receive if I complained of her conduct.

I woke early and looked around the plantation. Its routine, like so many I had seen, was suppressive and comical to a degree. Van Halm, fully recovered from the night's indulgences, was the principal actor in the pantomime, for that name fitted it best. He was wearing the usual planter's morning dress, which consisted of a silken white open shirt with an inch of frill around the neck and fine white Holland trousers. Over that he wore a loose, light nightgown of expensive Indian chintz. On his head sat a gossamer nightcap, and resting like a crest upon that was an enormous beaver hat. A slave walked behind him with the Madeira and water at the ready. Van Halm carried in his own hand—wonder of wonders—his pipe, as faithful a companion as a favored dog. It was usual for Europeans to walk unencumbered at all times.

With a flourish he led us to a table groaning under the weight of fruit, cheese, coffee, buttered toast, and all that wealth provided daily and which was served to us by men and women who dared not eat even that which fell to the ground. The dogs competed for food with ants and flies, but never with slaves.

The overseer whose duty it was to attend Van Halm arrived and in a monotone recounted the jobs that had to be done that day. After that, the state of the plantation population was reviewed—the sick, the newborn, the runaways, the lazy, the neglectful, the drunks. None were ever virtuous on any plantation I had visited. All miscreants were automatically found guilty, and the flogging began. Hempen cords were used to belabor the slaves and a "Danke, Massera" was demanded.

Van Halm was not in any degree affected by their cries. Moments passed and another character entered the scene, à dressy Negro with a serious air wearing what

75

appeared to me to be fancy dress. Van Halm railed and shouted at him for allowing sickness among the slaves.

"You black swine. Why for slaves get sick? Next time I'll kick you open like a rotten calabash. You feed them rice."

"Yes, Massera. Danke, Massera." He crept away like a beaten dog.

An old woman next appeared, behind her a chain of children. She was the superannuated matron, too old for fieldwork. The children were still dripping from their wash in the river. "Morning, Massera," they sang, clapping their hands. "God bless you, Massera. Danke for food. Danke, Massera."

The woman flicked her whip, and they ran off to stand meekly beside a large platter of cold rice and plantains. They dared not touch the food until the woman said, "Nyam." They ate meekly and smacked their lips in appreciation, as they were taught to do.

Van Halm had shown me fully the power of the planter over those at his mercy. In such an idyllic place I was surprised to find this naked harshness and blind degradation of the human heart. No wonder Cecily, the girl I had chosen, never smiled. Three times I had tried to make her respond as a woman should, but there was nothing in her that was gentle, loving, giving, and accepting of a European.

I gave up and went home to Joanna. She pushed me away from her when I tried to embrace her, and I could see thunder and lightning in her beautiful face. It had a special glow when she was angry.

"What is the matter?" I asked, imagining that yet another man or woman or child had insulted her, as so often happened. "You look so miserable—so unhappy. Is there anything that offends you?"

In a scarcely audible tone she said, "I do not know you well, and when I do I hate it. You talk up for the poor: give to them; help slaves, pity them. Yet you do not do right by women. Your mother is a woman. You come from one. Yet you do not respect them. You pull them into a crab hole and you go there, too. You cover them with filth. You're all the same. What is a gentleman? What does such a man do that is not the same as a bad man? You make me think that every day is a day of slavery."

I was completely taken aback. "How do you speak, Joanna. How so?"

"Which poor woman was it last night?" she sobbed. "Which poor slave girl who you took like a biscuit, like a glass of wine, like anything else? Whom did you pull about, drink down, spill, throw away, since you left here?"

"Joanna," I said smoldering. "You dare to question my actions? You are not to trouble yourself about me."

"Yes," she replied. "I want to know why, when you are with white men, you do as they do? Why you become like them? You have to be the best fighter, lover, singer, dancer! Stop betraying yourself and their wives!"

"What do you expect me to do, madam? Be a brawny idiot like your Uncle Cojo, who wears a bracelet with 'Faithful to the Europeans' written on it to save his skin and who shoots monkeys for food? You question my actions?"

"Yes, I do. If you prove rotten and evil, I will die." She placed her head in her hands and sobbed. "It's a sickness with you. Like the *belly-hatty*. When you get it you run to the bush. Do you not know slave women also understand fidelity and are also capable of joy and pain?"

The whole room was overspiced with a fog of pain and distrust. After a few minutes she gave me a long, sweeping look and departed. After she had gone I thought of all that she had said. Even in her anger she was unlike anyone I had ever known, and I had known swarms of women of all shapes and sizes. Loving them had been truly like any other sport for me. I was in a state of panic as I thought of our love shattered like glass upon stone, broken like eggshells and useless, like roses in a winter frost.

Van Halm came to fetch me once again to his plantation, Sporkesgift, but I declined.

"By the way," he said, "Cecily got two hundred lashes today. She tried to knife my overseer."

"What did he do to her? She was a perfectly nice girl in my opinion," I said.

"Do you think I ought to sell her?"

"Yes, I would ask Zubbly Sampson to buy her! I'm going to Fauconberg now, and I will write to Zubbly Sampson tomorrow. She is at her tobacco plantation."

"Why don't you bring Joanna to Sporkesgift with you?"

"No, good Van Halm. That would not be possible."

"It is amazing how a man of your stature submits to a slave!"

"Not to a slave, Van Halm. To my wife." I watched him go and then, calling Quaco, left for Fauconberg.

Joanna was with the accountant in his office preparing the list of provisions at the request of Mr. Lolkens, who left such things to her. Beatrice was there, too. I could see that they had both been crying.

"I have come to take you home," I said.

She shrugged. "I am at home, Captain. Here at Fauconberg." She never called me John, and only when she wanted to tease me did she address me as "Massera."

"You understand what I mean, Joanna. I entreat you. Come home with me."

"I will think of it while I am working. And there's Bea here, too. She might be happy of this chance to talk with you. If you should need to drink, Mr. Lolkens is in his bookroom."

I went into the garden and was sitting quietly drawing some flowers when a pretty little African child dressed in the Dutch style came by. She curtsied and walked over to where some other children worked at weeding the paths. They sang as they worked, as the adults did, only their song was more of a poem in the mouth of a white child. These children worked for long hours and helped their own parents tend the small gardens behind their huts. The plantations supplied no vegetables or fruits, and the slaves either grew or bought what they needed. The best produce was kept by the overseers, who in return distributed rice, flour, salt fish, and salt pork or salt beef in stated quantities twice a year.

Joanna at last showed herself.

"Well, are you coming or shall I go home alone? I felt grossly insulted by you, madam!" I exclaimed.

She shrugged and all the way home she remained in a serious and contemplative mood. When we were in our own house I held her close. I could observe that although she desired me, she felt betrayed and bruised. I acted the true penitent, eager to throw myself at her feet and speak with sincerity on my own behalf. But what to say and how? I did not know. My eyes moved over her face, trying to find a hint of forgiveness.

"Oh, dear Joanna, to my sadness and shame your words are entirely true. Forgive me. You have made me think, and until I hear you say you forgive me, I would not impose myself upon you."

I took her hands in mine and felt her tremble at my touch. "Forgive me, dear Joanna. It was never my intention to cause you pain."

We lay in bed, so close-bound by our deep love. Her husky, accented voice sank to a dramatic whisper. "I know that you care, and when you stop caring—near or far apart—I know that there is no place in this world where I should want to be. Being European is not your color. It is what you do."

Gently she traced the length of my backbone with one finger. I turned and faced her. "Joanna, my dearest," I said, "come to my arms and once again into my heart."

I had slept while she cooked the meal. When I awoke we talked of the plantation.

"Is the girl Tamera Cojo's child?" I asked.

"No, he has none. When he dies they will bury him with the lower port of his body exposed. Since he has no children, he can have no shame in his body."

"Does he not have women?"

"I suppose so, but he fishes and shoots for the plantation and keeps out of trouble. At Fauconberg men, too, are told when and who."

"I did not know that."

"How could you? You are not one of us. It is what I fear most: that no matter how horrid, how drunk, how disgusting the man, I must obey. My father and Mrs. Demelly's mother shared the same parents. I will always be grateful for the way she protected me. I felt the eyes of the old whore-men on me, betting, talking disgusting,

thinking disgusting and wishing disgusting about me."
Then she added, "Tamera is Jolly Couer's daughter."

Jolly Couer, I had been told, was one of Baron's generals. Baron, one of the Cottica rebels, was known to be fierce and merciless. With Jolly Couer, he appeared at New Rosenback Plantation. Having tied the hands of Shults, the owner, and plundered the house, the Africans ordered the musicians to play the music of their masters: gavottes, quadrilles, and reels. He and his men danced and feasted until they decided to end Shults's existence.

Shults looked at Jolly Couer and pleaded, "Oh, Jolly Couer, remember the dainties I gave you from my own table when you were but a child, my favorite, my darling among so many others?"

"Oh, I remember," was the reply. "I remember how you ravished my mother and flogged my father when he tried to assist her. I looked on in horror, and you saw me weeping and damned my tears. Remember this and die by my hands!"

He severed Shults's head with a hatchet with one blow and played bowls with the head. He next cut the skin from the miserable man's back and spread the skin over one of the cannons to keep the priming dry.

We accompanied Beatrice home to La Marre's plantation and talked awhile with her owner, who had so many children.

"I am often asked how I remember them all," La Marre said calmly. "But I do. They have merely five mothers, each with four children. And my sweet Bea has none as yet."

We spent a lovely night there, all our arguments forgotten. We were as one again and very much in love.

We did not hasten to return to L'Esperance. But when I did, I learned that Fourgeoud, before leaving Paramaribo on leave, had given me permission to build a family house and have Joanna to be with me as long as I liked. I was greatly relieved, as the hut at Hope was too small for us I began to look forward to a quiet life in a pleasant spot with my lovely wife, my boy Quaco, and a firm resolution never again to take liberties with Joanna's trust in me.

I brought all my resources together. They amounted to two sheep, twenty hens, and a pig, two hundred florins, and provisions for our food. I was so happy I bought a hat with gold lace for Quaco. The flowers of my garden showed good color, and I thanked God for his mercies, which included the eggs laid by the colonel's hens, two of which I filched to make my posset,* my hens having laid no eggs as yet. Joanna went down river to Fauconberg, and I was able to hear Quaco recite his letters and spell the few names of the creatures he had learned—easy words such as *bird, egg, star,* and *water,* which showed that small brain or no brain, he was capable of learning. At this time there was much talk as to whether Africans were human at all; souls and the ability to think and reason were not attributed to them, although many were capable craftsmen of immense abilities often confounding such low beliefs about them.

I hung my hammock high above the mosquito line as once directed by old Camaraca, and was at the point of going to sleep when I heard a weeping and caterwauling rather like that emitted by cats in heat. I leapt down among the mosquitoes only to find that our Berbician

---

*An eggnog made with ale or wine.

Captain Ackera had found his brother, Julius, a soldier among the Society Troops. They had been separated during a raid and had given each other up as dead, and now Fate had reunited them. They hugged and cried and gave news of others they had known, but the best news was that Ackera's wife and child were in Paramaribo. I was so touched by their tale that I offered two bottles of wine in celebration and called a toast to everyone's future happiness.

After a few days of peace the rebels were on the move again and I went off again on patrol to Alkmar, the Godefrooy plantation, where the slaves were so blissfully happy. Joanna wrote to say she was unwell each morning, and I suspected from the symptoms she described that she had caught. It was a wonderful message to receive. I was excited and pleased at the blessed thing that had happened to us, but my child would be a slave—outside my jurisdiction, as if he or she had crossed the ocean from the Guinea coast of Africa. When Joanna came to reside in the splendid little house of manicole palm, with the furniture also of manicole palm, all built by the slaves at L'Esperance out of love and affection for her, she was in full bloom. She settled into her home, which consisted of a parlor and dining room, a bedchamber where we stored luggage, a kitchen set away from the house, and a poultry house. It wasn't a mansion, but in it I was perfectly happy with the woman I loved. We walked and talked and sat among the flowers. I read to her—sometimes my own poems and sometimes from great poets of my youth. I read Donne's beautiful poem "The Exstasie" aloud to my love:

"Where like a pillow on a bed,
A pregnant bank swelled up
The violet's reclining head,
Sat we two, one another's best.
Our hands were firmly cemented
With a fast balm, whence thence did spring
Our eye beams twisted, and did thread
Our eyes upon a double string.
So to enter graft our hands
Was all the means to make us one."

I told Joanna of my boyhood days in Scotland, where I was sent for my education to my uncle, Dr. Stedman. He taught me nothing, but one Jack Chambers, my principal companion, taught me everything that was wicked, all of which displeased the righteous household. I returned home labeled as incorrigible and on my way to the gallows.

I continually fought and was the prime instigator of all hurly-burly and street battles. When expelled from school yet again, I learned to play the violin from one of the first players in Europe, a man named Farras. Twice a week I played at the dancing assemblies he held, and I fell in love at about fourteen years old with the admiral's daughter, Anna Van der Von, whom I many times dueled over with my feet and fists. Joanna listened as if in a state of trance. I was describing a world she never knew or ever could know.

Joanna's father, like mine, had loved her and taught her to play the spinet and sing and read in German and French and High Dutch. But his death had ended all that, and she now lived a lowly life. Once more she sighed and regretted her servitude, but for the moment that was the way of things. Our son would be born a Fauconberg slave.

When the colonel returned from his leave, we invited him to dine. I, rather than Joanna, knew of his charmless Swiss ways, his beady-eyed spite, and his tongue that could stir up more unrest than village wives. But when he saw my home and my wife, he was not only civil but positively charming to her.

"Such a fine woman, Stedman," he said. "She does you proud. Such a pretty girl but yet a slave."

Patronizing or not, he displeased me with his comments.

Joanna was so beautiful, I felt that oncoming motherhood increased her relationship with all nature.

The rains began and thundered down each night. She began to feel unwell due to the presence of flies and other bugs that came with the weather. The old Indian woman who always attended us in illness visited each day with potions to ease childbirth and accompanied Joanna to the Fauconberg Plantation, where her mother anxiously awaited her.

Orders came for us to march to the Wana Creek, and this gave an opportunity to see something of the variety of the plantations. The sailing between plantations lightened the burdens of the men and turned my thoughts from Joanna's childbed. The weather had rotted our clothes and shoes, and there were none to be bought on the riverbanks. The men were unkempt and foul-smelling and in rags, and often slaves took pity on them and fed them.

I sometimes witnessed the most unbelievable and ingenious forms of cruelty. The plantations were being bought by Americans fleeing from the War of Independence and its aftermath, and some of the American women refined the tortures the slaves already knew. No slave could defend his family for fear of loss of limb or life. The first object of my compassion during one visit was a beautiful African tied up by both arms to a tree. She was as naked as the day she came into the world and lacerated in such a shocking manner by the whips of two drivers that she was from her neck to her ankles dyed in blood. Her crime? She had firmly refused the embraces of her detestable tormentors.

I returned to L'Esperance to learn that Joanna had been delivered of a fine boy. I was so elated that I wrote letters to all my friends telling of the birth of my son John, whom we decided to call Jack. I received congratulations from all except my mother, who thought that I had degraded a worthy family; Joanna was a slave, and as far as my mother was concerned, they were the lowest creatures on God's earth.

Our colonel had his say, too, wishing that the child would not have my ludicrous disposition, which Captain Federicy passed on to me.

The colonel was at that time away in the woods after Bonny's hide. But while he hunted Bonny in one part of the woods, Bonny was at Killestyn Nova, another plantation, using a captured mother and her child as bait for his enemies. Unfortunately, the child was taken by a jaguar. Some free Africans rescued the woman, distraught and wandering in the bush, and brought her to L'Esperance. Bonny managed to set a plantation on fire with the director in it and cut off the leg of a mixed-race child.

Fourgeoud returned and while waiting for Bonny to show had trapped and caught two beautiful macaws, which I immediately tried to draw. But his valet de chambre exclaimed, "No! Stedman, no! No! They are for Her Highness, a present from the colonel. Leave them alone!"

"Just allow me a closer look. Just a little closer look,"
I said.

He opened the door just a trifle too wide, and one of
birds, the hen, grasped its freedom and flew away.

Fearing his ire, I ran and hid among the shrubs, and
I discovered a most beautiful sight. I had planted cress
to form Joanna and Jack's names, and they had grown
so well they could clearly be seen. I could overhear the
colonel swearing and demanding my head in the most
diabolical fashion for losing his bird, but then he suddenly swept himself up like a prima donna and placed a
banana beside the macaw in the cage. Not long after, the
hen returned to share the banana with her mate.

It reminded me of my gentle mate, and I planned to
write a most impassioned request to purchase Joanna. In
a fit of generosity, the colonel gave me leave to go to
Fauconberg. For the first time I saw my beautiful son
being bathed in wine and water, as was the custom. There
was much merriment and feasting and the slaves danced
because the father of the child had come. I wrote to
Messrs. Passelage and Son, the men who owned my wife
following Du Bois's bankruptcy, and offered a substantial
sum for her. I also wrote of the injustice that one human
being was owned by another and the descendants of that
person, and more, forever and ever, amen. My thoughts
on the slave trade were dire, but the writing had to be
done and the fact of the matter accepted: I would buy
Joanna if I had to live on water, salt, and bread forever.
I told them of her kindness to me in my illness. Mr. Lolkens, their administrator, supported me in every en-
deavor by appealing to his friends for the acceptance of
my terms.

I spent the rest of my time at Fauconberg drawing
my olive-skinned son with the burnished brown hair and

the bright blue eyes. He was adorable and adored by all who saw him. I returned to L'Esperance with joy congealed inside me and to the woods a happy man.

Early one morning at the camp at Hope where I had a small hut, we heard the report of several minute-guns in the direction of the Pirica River, as though aid were being summoned. I dispatched a detail and on its return learned that the rebels had been repulsed at a nearby plantation and that Fourgeoud had been within shouting distance of the rebels. The rebels nearly died of laughter as he shouted to his men. "Don't kill them. Take them alive."

Federicy said the laughter was at his throat and in his eyes.

"You crassy, Bakera!" the rebels yelled back. "We want *sootoo* you. We chop you to meat. We give you to pig to eat."

Eventually Federicy, although Swiss like Fourgeoud, could no longer conceal his laughter at the encounter, and tears of mirth ran down his face, gilded by the sun. It was good to see this man who had taken Boucou, a settlement the rebels valued, laughing so merrily. "There was the old man behaving as he would in his own country. He would take prisoners and then question them! I found it such splendid fun." Then Federicy grew serious, adding, "But when Fourgeoud wanted to be a good soldier, he was excellent. He went every step of the way with his men, regardless of the hazards. And it didn't matter how many rebels called him a bewhiskered *pingo* with a long nose!"

"Hey! Ho, damn!" a voice called from a tent boat. Mr. Ebber stepped on land, a barrel-shaped waddling man of woeful countenance. He had dropped in on the colonel to replenish himself and to receive sympathy for being fined after murdering a slave by prolonged and terrible tortures. The visitor's tyranny was renowned; it was joked about, derided, extolled, and regretted, but no one ever told him to his face about the evil of his deeds. He had driven a fourteen-year-old boy to madness because the boy appeared ugly to his eyes. He used his own diabolical system that the slaves feared with all their heathen hearts. They called the overseer Papa Diablo or Father Devil.

He had flogged the poor boy each day for a month after he'd tied him down flat on his back with his feet in the stocks. Then they had put an iron triangle around his neck so he could not escape or sleep except by sitting down; finally Mr. Ebber chained the boy to a dog kennel with orders to bark at every boat that passed. Eventually the slave boy died and Mr. Ebber was fined.

Mr. Blunderman, his successor, was marginally better. He began his improved reign by flogging the entire plantation of slaves because they had overslept for fifteen minutes. But Mr. Blunderman paid dearly. The slaves had been driven to desperation and decided to make a stand against the tyranny. One man, a Demerara River slave called Quashi, locked the door one morning when Mr. Blunderman was out of his house admiring the garden. The slave took the three children to the roof and threw them, one by one, into the courtyard. Then he cut his own throat. The system produced dangerous people on both sides and caused dreadful pressures to come between people and their humanity. The more I saw of these terrors, the more I was determined that my two loved ones would be saved from that life.

Although I was proud of my wife and bought her pretty dresses whenever I could, she was careful to be a slave girl in the presence of the mistresses—neither sitting nor being familiar nor laughing nor talking in their presence or on equal terms with them. Her hair had grown with Jack's birth and fell in a shower around her neck, but she took pains to wear braids, although under my guidance she had laid aside the attire of the mixed-race woman. She particularly trembled in the presence of one woman, Miss Goatzee, and I never took her on that plantation, even when she was invited.

Miss Goatzee, due to the war raging in that place, had come from Georgia with a weighty fortune and no husband. She accused me openly of disloyalty to my race. "The slave is a pretty creature, Mr. Stedman. But how would she be accepted in society?"

At other times she was even more alarming in her insinuations. Had I not given a promise to Joanna, I would have taught her a lesson or two—provided I could place a bag upon her head to hinder the sight of her teeth, like gravestones that had been ill served by the weather.

When I passed Miss Goatzee's plantation one day there were signs of the rebels. This threw the woman into a merciless passion. Calling upon her old cook to fetch her some condiment, she hit the old woman across the face with her riding crop because "too much time had passed" since she had requested the condiment.

Her favorite slave, a girl called Yettee, reminded her mistress that the old cook had been sick. Miss Goatzee turned upon Yettee, beating her and ordering that her ankles be chained to her hips until further notice. Yettee could not understand what she had said that had caused so much harm. She had stated a fact. They were both in the debt of the other, mistress and slave, in simple truth; that was all she had said.

I heard Yettee weeping and thought I'd try to help her. After exchanging pleasantries with Miss Goatzee, I raised the matter of the weeping girl. "You cannot make people better by punishments. What pleasure can you take in a deformed young girl? Oh, fie!"

"I am a Calvinist, sir, and this girl showed the sin of pride. And now she has fallen upon her two bound feet and must travel quickly upon them to be flogged."

"Are you not making her a Christian by so much suffering? The lions that ate the Christians could take many forms, madam. Many times a day the screams of these people rise up to heaven. Why, at a Wanna Creek settlement there was even a slave crucified, and he lay of his own will upon the cross."

She peered excitedly out of the window. "Look," she cried, pointing in the direction of her stables. "The mules are about to set upon each other. The men are all gathered. Why, the betting would be worthwhile. Come, Mr. Stedman. To the mule fight."

"No, good lady, not while Yettee suffers."

"I know you have a a preference for slave girls. But I will see to my slave!"

"I have a preference for all beautiful women, madam, and as for my wife, she is inestimable. A good, gentle, intelligent woman who has borne me a fine son. Though she is a mulatto."

"I am glad you acknowledge that fact, sir. A mulatto!" Had I not been drawing Miss Goatzee on commission, I might have slapped her hard.

At her plantation it had become the sport to set the mules to fight, as Gypsies sometimes set their horses. It was usually a social occasion, and the betting was often quite fierce. But Miss Goatzee had made it her sport with all the drinking and hallooing! She busied herself about joking and bantering as did not become her pretence at being a fine lady.

After a few minutes she returned to me. "Good sir," she said. "It will not do to sulk. Yettee has been released and stands on her two feet again."

But I ought to have known better. I took her arm as if she had been a courtesan, and we strolled to the entertainments. As the mules kicked and bit, Yettee ran among them, her eyes demented. They kicked and bit at her in a devilish synchrony. A scream. A cry. A groan and again a cry, and poor Yettee had collapsed.

"Water! Water!" she moaned. A slave bent over, trying to give her water.

"No!" exclaimed Miss Goatzee. "Let her die for her pride."

I ran to Yettee and snatched the gourd, intending to make her drink, but she was already past all hope. She had been accused of insolence by one of her mistress's friends and, anticipating her fate, had chosen death.

Later I was at pains to capture poor dying Yettee in my drawing and also Miss Goatzee, showing her cruel heart as though it had been her beautiful face. "Mr. Steadman!" she exclaimed, when I showed it to her among genteel company. "I now have room in my household for a mulatto. Will you sell me your wife? Better men have sold wives and children for ready cash." She tried in this manner to reduce me to inconsequence.

I gave her a long, hard, and piercing look. "Purchase my wife by any means whatsoever and I shall surely kill you. You evil white witch. May the devil take you," I said.

Five

Joanna had written to say she would return to the camp at Hope as soon as the pain of Jack's teething had abated. I had more time then to draw animals that the slaves and Indians brought in each day. I had by now quite a collection of strange birds and beasts that would be of interest to those who knew of them but had not actually seen them. My drawings, I was sure, would disprove some of the fanciful accounts that travelers to foreign parts had repeated without having verified them.

So there I was, engaged to the full in drawing, when I heard several shots in the distance. The rebels had come, I imagined, and instead of my blunderbuss I had a pencil in my hand. I listened. It came again: the sound of shots in quick succession.

I ran down to the river's edge and saw something heavy and black turning and rolling as it was carried along by the waves. It was in effect not a dead rebel, as I had imagined, but a dead manatee or sea cow that, like a whale, fed its young on milk. We pulled it ashore and, after I had drawn it, the Africans shared the meat, which was very like pork, among themselves. There was a hole in its side; it had apparently been shot by the rebels and lost before it could be retrieved.

It came suddenly amongst us and brought a brief merriment to the men, but soon the Angel of Death followed and attached itself to the entire force. Captain Van Heusen, with whom I had once fought, was killed the very next day in a rebel trap. Laurant had gone of the dysentery, and none of us could help pondering our own mortality. I tried to keep my body free of disease by exercising when we were told to camp, when bound by the weather, or when my fingers rebelled against drawing, painting, or making the baskets the Africans had taught me to make for dear Joanna and other friends. We patrolled the Cottica River, and as long as I did not find that wearying I imagined my health in good shape and pleasing to me. Joanna loved swimming, too, and after she arrived we often went out together to enjoy the river and its age and its mystery.

And then one morning I took a chill. It happened in a moment, and by afternoon I lay shivering and yet so hot an egg could have been poached upon my back. I conjectured that it would pass, so trifling it seemed to me. But it did not pass. Joanna was at her wit's end, as Fourgeoud was due to arrive at Hope with the physician to inspect the camp. The physician was a rather pompous little man who was packed with fat and anomalies. As soon as Fourgeoud arrived, Captain Kant informed him of my condition and apologized that I was not there in person. Not an instant was wasted questioning the authenticity of my condition. Instead, Fourgeoud hastened Mr. Steger to my bedside, and the great man at once proceeded to examine me in a most flamboyant manner.

"Show the tongue," he ordered. "Diseases of the internal organs of the abdominal regions indicated," he muttered, reaching for my pulse. "Weak!" he said. "Dying! Almost dead! He must be strongly physicked!"

He gave me one of his own concoctions, labeled "certain-to-be-effective." I could read the label at a distance. It said "certain to cure" in French.

The moment I swallowed it, I fell in a swoon to the ground. Joanna shrieked for Quaco, and they lifted me onto the bed. And there, I heard later, I lay for four whole days. But Steger had not yet concluded his adventure through my constitution. He passed me as dead, and Fourgeoud at once ordered that a nice, deep grave be dug for me.

My wife was distraught. She sent Quaco for cures from Graman* Quacey and also for medicines from Sara, the Indian woman. They kept a vigil around the hours, constantly rubbing my limbs with rum and imploring my soul not to leave my body. As far as I could recall, I was in dreamland, a child again playing with Willie and talking with my father as I used to do. My kind Scottish cousins were there, too, in this place where there were so many flourishing and appealing birds and flowers and slaves attended by their masters. In one corner was a bright light, but who tended it I could not tell. I wandered in, a small boy who bowed to everyone, and played my violin and then wept because I could not see my mama. A crowd gathered round me and there was weeping and singing and then I levitated—up, up I rose above the bed and toward the window, but I could not get out, the window being too small for my size. I began to fall and landed once more upon my bed.

Smelling the odor of wet wood, I blinked. The strong light troubled my sight, but I could discern my darling wife. She threw herself upon me and sobbed.

Quaco stood beside me, shaking me and asking, "Massa, you go drink rum—a little bit?" His face was bathed in tears. "Rum, Massa?"

"No!" came a voice I recognized as Camaraca's. "Captain go drink dis."

---

*Great man.

"No," I told them all. "All I need truly and deeply is tea."

Joanna brewed me some tea as I had taught her, and I lay there to receive her care and her love.

"Where did Camaraca come from?" I asked weakly. "He was in hospital at Cofaay last time I saw him. I thought he had been killed."

"No, Cap'n, Camaraca no dead. Camaraca plenty live," Camaraca said.

When I was able to sit outside, Colonel Fourgeoud visited. "You have nine lives, Cap'n Stedman," my colonel said. "I feared for your life this time." He mentioned nothing of the coffin that had been made and the grave that had been dug for me on his instructions. I was so weakened by my illness that I was allowed a long period of convalescence at Egmond, the plantation of Monsieur Cachelieu, where the air was fine and good. Cery still took care of Johnny, so Joanna was able to accompany me and love me in that soothing way she had.

Monsieur Cachelieu entertained us there. He was a strange man, putting great importance on physical beauty and youth. The old and the ugly were especially heavily punished. When I pointed out that beauty is but skin deep and old age comes to all, he said, "Never to me, Monsieur Capitaine. I shall put a bullet to my 'ead long before old age comes to cripple me."

Had he not thought my Quaco good-looking—as he certainly was, so finely worked by the Almighty's hand were his features—I would have been forced to refuse Cachelieu's hospitality. But all was well and when he beheld Joanna he praised her bearing and her composure.

He was much given to practical jokes at the expense of his slaves. He insulted one of his neighbors by letter, and in reply, the poor slave who delivered the letter was given four hundred lashes to take to his master. Cachelieu thought that an entertaining story, and so did many of his friends.

His plantation was superbly planned, with light and shade and lakes and with layers of quiet places full of exotic flowers. The soil was excellent and produced luscious fruit and wines that were kind to the nose and the digestion. It was a heavenly place except for the cries that regularly filled the air when the whipping began.

I found much to draw, and Joanna worked quietly at her embroidery and her lace, thus avoiding the cruel talk and idle chatter of the mistresses and the slaves.

Passelage, the owner of Fauconberg, had died before answering my letter concerning my purchase of Joanna's freedom, and I was seized with anxiety when I realized that Fauconberg would once more be sold. This time my son would be there, with the possibility of permanent separation from us if he were bought out of pique or spite. I appealed to Fourgeoud for leave to go to Paramaribo to ascertain who had been appointed to manage Fauconberg, but he refused my request and my misery became unbearable. A continual flow of all the horrors I had seen passed before me, and I became so depressed sleep was impossible. But I need not have worried so. De Graav, whom I had known well since coming to Surinam, became administrator representing Mr. Lude, who had bought Fauconberg. De Graav was a planter and owner of the beautiful and successful plantation La Bonheur. He was a fair man to his slaves and very discreet and sensitive in his extramarital activities. In the question of my dear wife he was most obliging, and all was well.

At this time Kennedy, from whom I had borrowed Quaco, asked for him to be returned. I dispatched Quaco at once with a letter offering to purchase him for five hundred florins, which Mrs. Godefrooy advanced me, and by God's grace and the willingness of Quaco's owner, my offer was accepted, and the loyal, faithful Quaco was mine. I welcomed him with open arms when he returned and drank to his future one day in freedom.

I had written a letter Quaco was told to post to Breda, where lived my mother, who was bitterly opposed to Joanna. The letter contained drawings of Joanna and our son. Although my mother praised Johnny's good looks and the beauty of his mother, she still suggested that I should marry a girl from a good family, since I had not made my fortune in almost five years. This annoyed and upset me—mainly because of its veracity.

I was expected to join Colonel Fourgeoud at Magdenburg encampment and arrived there with other officers. The estates were now few indeed, unexpected little islands among the verdure, many in ashes and the others accommodating the timber-cutters. Magdenburg was a desolate, barren, and ghostly settlement. There were only soldiers there and a few Africans to carry the luggage and help in the military barges.

Some of the men hated the Africans and used them most cruelly. One day, a hundred slaves arrived, and as we sailed, one guarding the military barge was missed. I investigated and found some fresh bloodstains in the barge. We arrested the two soldiers who had been with him in the barge and charged them with murder. If they were found guilty, I would shoot them.

Nine days later, a provision barge coming down from Paramaribo found the poor slave half dead in the bush, his throat cut from ear to ear. The knife of the two culprits had missed his windpipe. Our physician, Mr. Crobaert, sewed up the wound, and the man recovered and was sent with a shipload of others back to his plantation.

I had noticed how social the monkeys were, living and letting others live. But not so men. Some of the soldiers were so vile I preferred the monkeys.

There were many fascinating species of monkeys, as different from each other as man from man, but lacking only the power of speech. It was a release to watch their antics and forget the life of the camp and to walk in the bush and discover the orchids and butterflies that were so numerous. The squirrels were also inquisitive and noisy, some with wings that, by nature's skill, caused them to fly.

We marched for a few days but saw no rebels and so returned to Magdenburg to find September, the captured rebel, dead from dropsy. Fourgeoud had instructed the poor man on pain of death always to follow him. This he did as a faithful dog would, but no amount of cajolery, bribery, or attention by questions or hard labor would persuade September to break the oath he took to his group.

The Dutch had exploited the whole of the west coast of Africa, an area stretching from Cape Verde to Angola. As a result, Africans from the whole coastal area formed the slave population of Surinam. The greatest number came from the Guinea coast; and we had amongst us Abos from the Cameroon; Conia from the Senegal; Blitay from Togoland; Coromantin, Ashanti, and Wassa from the Gold Coast; Gango and Mandingo from Sierra Leone; Ibos, Nagas, and Yorubos from Nigeria; and Pombo from the Congo. The Lokomen or priests or Obeahmen, evil wizards, bound the tribes together by oaths of loyalty—the one common element in their belief about the nature of life, disease, and God. But with their absolute power over slaves, the planters turned these different tribes against each other. They placed in the minds of the natives their own patterns of right, suspicion, mistrust, and hatred, and encouraged them to ignorance and superstition. We had caught September, a virile, supple, reckless man who could swim with a blunderbuss held above his head using just his feet and one hand. When he died he was worn out and bloated, murdered as surely as if he had been shot—murdered by bad food, maltreatment, and hatred. All ignored his cries, but I was sure they stayed forever in the ears of God.

Each day my foot became a trifle more tender and swollen; the slaves urged me to find out who had cast a spell upon me, as they believed all illness was sent by others. My foot became so painful I could not walk upon it. In addition, the fatigue from the heat made me short of breath and extremely bad-tempered. I was further aggravated by the constant row taking place between the African rangers, freed Africans trained to track rebels, and the soldiers. The rebels had killed some rangers and stolen their red hats (their only distinguishing mark, being themselves as black as the rebels, who wore their hair plaited closed to their skulls). The loss of the red hats concerned us all, as the sight of them would hinder our attack upon a man approaching us in such attire. The soldiers reproached the rangers as poltroons and traitors and also as being deliberately in partnership with their relations, the rebels. The rangers challenged their tormentors to single combat and accused them of stealing a leg of pork. The soldiers continued with the same accusations; they had owned the pork, they swore, although we all knew they had taken the Africans' pork as a right.

I investigated the theft of the pork and, in as solemn a manner as I could muster, threatened the soldiers with a bastinading and the rangers with a whipping at precisely two o'clock. The peace that came over the camp was like the peace of heaven. At two o'clock I limped out and summoned all the men—some already in tears. I held in my hand the large leg of pork and commanded that it be cleft in two, a larger and a smaller piece. I gave the larger piece to the Africans and said that if I heard so much as a whisper about the pork, the hats, or any other single word upon such matters, there would be such a performance as would please the devil.

"Three cheers for Cap'n Stedman," both sides shouted, and off they went, some to play reels upon the fifes and dance upon the grass, the others to play upon their drums.

Whether it had been the vexation of my discourse with the men or the state of my constitution I do not know, but I was quite unable to stand upon my foot at all, and fearing amputation of the limb, I was at once sent downriver to Paramaribo. I was taken to La Marre's residence, where Joanna and Johnny were visiting Beatrice. Joanna at once sought remedies from whichever source she could. An eminent physician was called and bled me twice, but though the fever and pain had disappeared, I still could not walk. Van Schouten, who had newly come to Surinam and was rich, came to visit and gave me an airing in his chaise; with Johnny and Joanna, I enjoyed myself thoroughly.

Pleased to see me regaining my strength, Joanna gave me news of the rebels, who had taken all the women from the Blue Bergh Estate, with Bea adding that she wished they would come and take three of La Marre's wives whom she heartily disliked.

Fed up with the women's talk, I attempted to walk for the first time in a week to take an airing. The stoutness engendered by the diet of soldiers had gone from me, and though I felt strange at first, I was able to walk. With a merry heart I journeyed to De Graav's house.

I had forgotten that Miss Spaan's house, where the greatest cruelties occurred each day, adjoined De Graav's home. And on that day, when my heart was full of pleasantries, I saw her with her own hands beat a slave across the breast principally because she laid temptation upon the male slaves.

De Graav received me with much sympathy, and so did another visitor, Bolls, who implored my advice on how to dispute his love for Mimi against his deep love for Mary without parting from either. All the while cries of slaves under the lash came from Miss Spaan's residence to mingle with our merriment.

De Graav, angered by it all, said, "The more she tortures her slaves, the more men shun her, and the more she is shunned, the more she needs blood and bones and souls—even though they are black ones." I agreed wholeheartedly. Soon enough the talk turned to the oncoming Mulatto Ball. I had forgotten that Joanna and I were invited to a dance to celebrate Graman Quacey's return from Holland.

Graman Quacey arrived at the dance dressed in a suit of blue and scarlet trimmed with gold lace. On his hat he wore a white feather, and he was the very copy of a Dutch general. This African, with extraordinary gifts, not only obtained his freedom from the state of slavery but, by his ingenuity and artfulness, earned a very good living. He was renowned as a Lokoman or ritual priest among the slave population, who believed so much in his Obeah and his charms that they thought he could discover the perpetrators of any crime. His amulets cost money, but slaves and planters, heathens, Christians, and Jews, bought them. But what he made most money from was his discovery of powerful febrifuge, a root of the Quascia bitters, to which, as the first discoverer of a cure for malaria, he gave his name, Quacey, corrupted to Quasia. He was an old man and said he had acted as drummer and beaten the alarm on his master's estate during the French occupation of the colony of Surinam in 1712. His head was gray in a full and flourishing way, and he stood, a rotund and bulging object, to receive his guests.

The Prince of Orange had given Graman Quacey expensive presents of goodwill after Quacey had placed before His Highness the cruelties of the planters to their slaves. His Highness had promised that those who landed at Texel, a seaport, and there remained for six months or, if their masters requested, a year would be free men.

The show of affection and loyalty for the guest of honor at the party was considerable. There were many mulattoes, and the dances were decorous and genteel. The women with their fashionable dresses and beautiful faces shone in double splendor. The music was spirited and correct such that I felt no strangeness among these people, who possessed much of the manners and refinements of their masters and mistresses, who in some cases would have done well to take examples of speech and decorum from their slaves.

Joanna wore the white silken gown she had worn on our wedding day nearly three years before, but through her womanly skills she had enriched it with a show of roses round the waist. She looked so enchanting with her modest grace and bearing, her hair so tastefully fixed, her charm a lantern in the room. Many of the women wore elaborate wigs, which in some cases contrasted markedly with their smooth, sable complexions.

I danced twice, once with my pretty and able wife and the other time with Zubbly Sampson, the bête noire of those whose credit notes she held. She had made a fan of them, and this she sometimes carried in public, much to the mortification of those who though envying her riches were forced by their bankrupt existence to borrow from her. She was an entertaining encyclopedia of scandal and gossip—yet as searching as the wind in January.

"I often think of Janus, good sir, when I see you," she said. "I inquire after your wife and also of your friends."

"All in good order, madam."

"Do you regret your absence from your beautiful country?"

"It is a distressing subject, madam. Being a soldier makes it so."

"Your wife's beauty speaks for itself. Let her not be a lonely and neglected one."

I bowed. "How was your stay in England, madam?"

"Full of excitement. The talk of abolition grows apace. I have met many people who seek our freedom, although mine had been bought for me. You see, marriage among slaves and Europeans was not the done thing. But my master left me wealth, and after three years of thinking about it, Zobre, his handsome business partner, wed me. There was much talk. Many counted my wealth besides him."

I had heard talk of it. "But gossip matters not," I said. "Where there is love, it matters not."

"You must visit us when my daughter Amelia comes home. She is a sweet child—a mere ten years of age."

She was a woman of commanding stature, with slender, fully extended bones. She held a cigar between long, delicate fingers and, bidding me adieu, went to wait upon the Great Man. She called for silence, and Graman Quacey told of his visit to His Highness the Prince, to whom he had made a case affecting the lot of the slaves.

"We shall be free," he promised. "One day soon we will be free."

"To freedom," I said. "Let us drink to freedom," and then stepped forward and bowed to that company of distinguished people.

I had enjoyed the ball, but somehow Joanna was depressed with all the talk of freedom and the time to come. I took both her hands and kissed them in gratitude for her kindness.

"Be patient," I said. "You will be free."

I had then a thousand florins in my pocket, having just had my pay and a lucky day gaming, and although my foot ached again with the dancing, I scrambled out on crutches, taking with me all the money I had in the world, to Mrs. Elizabeth Godefrooy. I paid her the five hundred florins that were outstanding for Quaco and the rest toward the two thousand florins that Joanna, priced at one-twentieth part of the estate, would cost me to purchase.

When Joanna heard of it, she was adamant in her refusal to exchange one benefactor to the interest of another.

"Here I am among my own people. Among your people I would be Joanna the rescued slave girl, shunned and despised by your friends and family. No, Captain John, our happiness is dearer to me than life, but it would never have any weight until my liberty had been earned or fairly bought to the last fraction of a florin. We will only be apart for a year or two, when you will leave the army, and then you will come for me. We must bear this tribulation—I like a woman and you like a man. Mrs. Godefrooy, at my request, will not accept your money."

She looked me over fully, as if uncertain of something, then embraced our child, turned from me, and began to weep most bitterly.

At that moment news reached us that La Marre had quite suddenly died. Joanna and I hastened to add our sorrow to that of the family. What would become of the twenty children he had sired, both white and mixed-race—all a potpourri on the plantation? He had always been a worthy brother-in-law. Beatrice sat sobbing—so young she looked to face bleak widowhood. I sat beside her, but she spoke not, nor did I.

Suddenly she said, "He was such a good man. He knew it all—when to be my father or my brother or my man. There is a great wall of darkness in my head. And I so young."

Disasters seemed to come upon us as surely as the birds flew overhead. My foot, though healed, still ached, and in a state of intense turmoil I rose to leave. De Graav, who had also come, stopped and greeted me, and when Joanna unexpectedly entered the room he, in a proprietary manner, dismissed her.

A rush of anger, grief, and pique all together came upon my whole soldier's body, making it intense in heat and then in cold. "You are a respected and valued friend, good De Graav, but is it your call to dismiss my wife?" I asked in a passion.

"Here she is but a slave," he replied innocently.

"No, good De Graav. At Fauconberg perhaps. Everywhere else, she is my wife."

"I beg your pardon, good Stedman. But I have come upon business which concerns Joanna. I have this day manumitted Henry, her brother, and he will go to Holland soon. I came to say this and found death. I beg your pardon. I did not want her to hear of it from her mother, but from me after I had talked with you about the matter."

We shook hands upon the matter of Joanna, but I had made a stand against wealth, prosperity, and vanity and damned them all. The men saw the slaves as women only in the bedchamber. The European women kept for themselves the title of wife, and woe to those Africans who tried to attain it. Why, Mrs. Mycee, who needed to wear a pillow sack upon her ugly head and face, asked me in my wife's presence to supply the place of her husband.

"Madam," I had replied. "I will drink a physic nut emetic, eat a relish of Epsom salts, or pay court to a baboon, but your bedchamber, never. There is for me no accommodation where the petals have fallen."

She frowned deeply and then said, "I spoke in jest, sir. My husband is an honorable man."

That woman was like a child who used the slaves as dolls were used—to be destroyed, torn limb from limb and thrown to the flames. I could see from the way her eyes flitted over Joanna that she would purchase her simply to destroy her and that she would not balk at the most extravagant price for the pleasure.

But I had weightier problems to consider. How could I raise the money to purchase Joanna? It was not a great deal of money, but any amount is a great deal when it is not in one's purse. Every time I thought of the cruelties that were daily the lot of slaves I became agitated, and so I resolved consciously to set those thoughts aside.

On the Prince's birthday, Fourgeoud, who had come to town, entertained the officers with salt beef, salt pork, barley puddings, and hard pease—a diabolical concession to the men's appetites. I did not attend, even though I liked such gatherings.

I was so preoccupied I could not engage in any of the reels or country dances. Mrs. Godefrooy in a letter to me from her town house had refused to stand surety for my family. She could not bear to tell me, so she wrote. Nor would the good lady explain to me the reason why she would not stand surety. I could not get the idea of having displeased my benefactress out of my mind. I talked to Rhynsdorph, her son-in-law, about the matter and he confided that she had refused to be guarantor for two of his favorite slaves as well. She would give gold, but not her signature. She, however, advised me to consult with the governor in regard to Jack's manumission.

I lost no time in calling upon His Excellency, and his invitation to dinner allowed me to lay the matter before him. He promised me faithfully to lay my request before the court, although he could not say further about the outcomes of such matters.

I mentioned the Prince's promise to Graman Quacey in which the Prince had pledged freedom for those able to live in Texel for a year.

"I have not yet perused the account of the Prince's meeting with Great Man Quacey," the governor said. "But you, good Stedman, must attend the ball to be held at my Indigo Plantation, and we will speak of it then."

I always accepted invitations to plantations where I could see different species of animals to draw, as well as flowers and fruit of botanical interest, and the governor's plantation was a storehouse of nature. But I could not help pondering how the mass of slaves was treated, and the more I thought of it, the more I resolved that Johnny would never be so disregarded by any man.

The food upon which slaves were fed weakened their resistance to disease, yet they were worked to produce increasing wealth. Their children and their women could be taken at will, and they must submit to tortures such as flagellations and live burnings. The Congo tribes committed suicide by swallowing their tongues. Some chewed poisonous roots, the earth, or even insects that would kill them. But those acts enraged their masters and mistresses the more.

Throughout the colony, one-legged and one-armed men were common. Legs were lost for running away from persecution and hands for raising them against whites, however sore and unjust the provocation.

Fate must have read my thoughts, because as my boat reached the water behind the governor's house I came upon a little band of people who were no more than skeletons, newly arrived by ship and being taken to De Graav's plantation. They moved along the road in a random, labored way, a picture of utter misery and desolation. Behind them walked the slave dealer with a whip to urge these automatons to further effort. I recalled my son as I had left him—beautiful, well fed, and sparkling with energies of all kinds. A passage from the prophet Ezekiel came to mind, and I said as they passed me unseeing and in fear, " 'And the Lord caused me to pass by them round about, and behold, there were many in the open valley, and lo they were dry. And he said unto me, "Son of Man, can these bones live?" And I answered, "Oh Lord God thou knowest." ' "

I returned to my home and found my son fast asleep beside his mother. I kissed them both and then, after many years of never seeking God's guidance, prayed for Joanna's future out of slavery.

The colonel, knowing full well that I was still on furlough, wrote instructing me to join him at Magdenburg at once, where the men were all sick from the shortage of food. The number of casualties among them was high on account of the traps set by the rebels for us and the natural conditions in which the soldiers hunted the rebels.

Every single day men died of the scurvy and of the plagues of the forest—worms, scorpions, flies, ticks, the bush yaws, mosquitoes, centipedes, and swamp fever. Our men were sorely reduced in number when dear Elizabeth Godefrooy, upon hearing of our plight, sent us another barge full of the necessary food, medicines, and liniments.

Of all the animals, most like man I would name the ants: some species industrious, some destructive of whatever comes in their way. Both rebels and sick soldiers stood in the way of good government.

The colonel took more notice of his men than of the Africans, but they died less. I sought the reason for this and found that Africans, when thrown together without interference with their natural thought, need not be told to "love their neighbor as themselves." They shared even a single egg with one or several others, while our men shouted, "I have only one; it is for me alone!"

Of all, the most retaliative were the Berbician Africans, who would not be called "Negroes." During a revolt, they had no scruples against cutting up their mistresses in the presence of their masters and killed whole families with the venom they carried under their fingernails. Several estates had been the victims of their fury. But when pleased with the conditions under which they served their masters, they worked well. Although they showed love, they never kissed their own families, but served them instead without question. Our African soldiers and rangers were clean and so fond of water they swam daily, two or three times. They were spirited, brave, and patient men and of the most undaunted fortitude.

After the famine among the men had been halted, news came that rebels had once again been seen at Altona, a plantation on which the overseer had been shot and which had since been burned. I met Altona's director as I was sailing downriver, and he informed me of the Obeah that had been passed on the day of the overseer's funeral.

"I tell you, Stedman, had I not seen it with my own eyes, no man's word would have made me think it possible. Whatever we did, the poor man kept falling through the coffin, the bottom landing once beside him, once on top of him, and at another time flung away. The Africans said their compatriot, a slave named Jupiter who is accused of the murder, was innocent. He is only twenty years old. Fearing a revolt, we could not break him there. Will you take him to Paramaribo?"

"Where is the slave now?"

"Jupiter is as merry as a lark in the prison hut, joking and watching and singing with the children playing *soesa*."

"*Soesa?*"

"It's a game they play, alternately stepping, clapping and slapping their sides to a song about their food—*congotay,** gari,† fufu‡*—the fruit they eat, and their

---

*Plantain flour.
†Ground yam or cassava flour.
‡Pounded boiled plantain.

friends." And then he asked me again, "Will you take the man?"

Seizing a chance to see my friends and family, I readily agreed to take the slave Jupiter downriver, and he was ordered aboard.

I told him where he was going and advised him to prepare to meet his God of whatever kind, for killing a white man. He did not seem to mind. "God is good. Slave owners are evil. You have learnt good because your heart is for us," he said seriously. "I have been dead for many days. And I have been dead many times. I was almost caught breaking the curfew once and another time I was in a desperate situation. My mistress, in an effort to wound her husband, told me to embrace her. If I did as she ordered, I would be dead; if I did not, same death. So I jumped into the river and swam for my life. The rebels saved me and then I got away from them, passing as free thereafter. I have remained free and find myself in this predicament only by coming here. As a free man it is a different life. You look white men in the eye, and they are not gods. I am not a slave, yet they think that I am."

I handed him over at the courthouse and made my way to Fauconberg. As I passed an official notice board, I saw a notice regarding my son Jack and read it with great delight: "Any person or persons who could give any lawful objection why Robert Stedman (called Johnny, the quadroon infant son of Capt. John Stedman) should not be presented with the blessing of freedom, such person or persons must appear before the court by Jan. 1, 1777."

I knew it to be a formality, and I thanked God, because as I brought the young man Jupiter to his destiny, I thought of Johnny twenty years thence.

I thought of Joanna, too. A man who loves as I had done must have the strength to pursue it and the will to sustain it to the end, because each friend, each acquaintance, each hateful slave owner makes what he can of it in his own heart and with the tricks of his own experience. Joanna was a part of my life. I wanted her to share both light and shade with me. Wherever I was I always wanted her beside me, but differences of power and color came between us and our lives—the army life and my social European life—often caused her pain. My Joanna! What was she worth to me besides my despised, demented heart which I so freely offered to her: If we could but find a haven and sail to it on halcyon seas and there reside until old age or death came to find us still happy! And still in love! Until I found her I was game for love's exploits, but she had come as a tranquil sea to bring me peace! Was it because she was a slave that I loved her? No. She was chaste but not dispirited. She was silent, but how loudly her looks and her actions spoke!

I prayed for them both and bade evil ever to depart from them. Nothing is good about slavery, to a slave or to one who truly loves a slave.

Then I recalled the first time we slept together, her gentle touch upon my cheek, her head flirtatiously tilted, her eyes willing me to be tender with her. I held her, oh so closely, her warmth and her softness a fresh and tender background to her loving of me. I recalled her desire to be made wise, to give generously of whatever was hers, and our need to treasure those moments forever. We had talked of what lay before us, of what we should encounter and what overcome, having no idea of the enormity of it. She did not speak as a woman concerned only with immediate survival. She had dreams and hopes and thoughts.

She had placed my hand upon her heart and said, "When I think of you there is a greenness here. And when I dream there is a stirring here also."

I asked myself what fate had led me to that inestimable woman and what my life would have been without all that she said to me by her looks and her silences alone.

"Joanna," I often whispered, "you will be forever locked in my soul."

Six

In Surinam the dry weather brought forest fires that burned with such fury and duration that the whole colony was covered with a gray haze, making the dwellings and the landscape distant and mysterious. Only gradually did their true forms appear. The savannah on that morning was the stage set for a ghastly tableau of punishments, executions, or whatever else had been selected for the slaves by due process as understood by their overseers.

We had gathered, a motley crowd of Christians, Jews, and heathens, some to witness the just, and others the unjust, punishment of slaves. It was not unlike the gathering of the Roman populace to rejoice at the sight of Christians being mauled or devoured by hungry lions, only at this time and in this place the lions were the habits, customs, prejudices, and laws of the colony. I recognized the same blood lust, the same mindless hilarity and simmering barbarity I had seen in the London mobs as they thronged to Newgate and Tyburn. The closer the crowd came to the place of execution, the more eager its expectation of pleasure at the shedding of blood.

The slaves were no longer persons—just chattel. I thought of my Joanna, so lovely and so resigned to her fate, knowing that from some things no one could save her. She, like these poor, helpless people unable to argue or resist, had nothing that was entirely her own. She could think but never act, could feel but never react. There were but a few moments of her life to which she could lay claim: the moment of her birth, for she had to be born; the moment when she gave birth, as she could affirm it; and the moment when she would die. That moment she would recognize. In spite of my deep love for her, these were the times when I realized that our love, so ill regarded by the community, could lead us only to unhappiness and despair. My friends particularly saw our marriage as an unequal game, a purposeless philander, a wasted time—days, weeks, and even years of wasted time. But that was all a slave girl should expect. Anything else would only complicate matters and embroil us both.

First there occurred the beatings—the simple, necessary emollients that daily oiled the wheels of the plantation life. But today, for example's sake, a ten-year-old boy was to be publicly whipped. His name was David Douglas, which, even coming from the huge mouth of the hangman, released a memory in me. I recalled his father—a handsome, red-haired Scot who enthralled us with his skill at billiards and who danced a fine Scottish reel on St. Andrew's Day. He had never married, but before dying of the bloody flux at Devil's Harwar he had lived with Justine, whom he had failed to manumit; although he had served in the Society Troops for many years, his request for her manumission was refused. Today, for opposing a man who tried to do his mother ill, the child was to receive a hundred lashes.

They brought him in, hands tied behind his back, feet bound together, and hung him from the only tree in the savannah. This tree, a sand *koker* tree left there for this purpose, served only to make the place appear large and more solitary. As they suspended him I could see the strain of supporting his body in the muscles of his arms, but not a word did he utter.

The whipping started and the executioner, an eager man, worked with a precise relish for his task. The crowd was poised for the cries of pain. None came. The stick on which he was all this time biting suddenly fell upon the grass, and the wail of pain came at last. A murmur of satisfaction swept through the crowd. They began to count in unison: ninety-one . . . ninety-five . . . ninety-nine . . . one hundred. He was no longer a body, just a mangled mass of blood red flesh. They threw his body on the grass.

A man from the Jews' Savannah rushed over and knelt beside him, muttering a prayer for the descent of mercy and the preservation of a young life. The overseer came over, first kicking the Jew aside and then the body. It did not stir. The rabbi held the boy's wrist and began another prayer. Several eyes looked down at him. At the end of the prayer the rabbi murmured, "He is dead now. He was so young, so kind. He would have become a fine man. I knew his father. God help us at this wicked time."

At this time the Jews had many privileges and their own settlement, the Jews' Savannah, where they kept up their ceremonies and traditions and where they could be sent for confinement if crimes outside their area were proved against them. They sometimes gave refuge to the slaves.

"How disappointing the child did not survive," said a woman in an elaborate wig. "It is so amusing to see them rise up with the blood a pattern of ribbons upon them."

Next came the slave I had brought down to the courthouse to be tried. Jupiter came striding into the savannah carrying the cross on which he was going to be *spansbockoed,* a dreadful punishment and different from the *spambock.* Naked as the day he was born, he looked around him with a scowl, as much as to say, "Barbarians! Dogs!" And then, realizing the futility of escape, he lay down upon the cross. The executioner, hatchet in one hand, crowbar in the other, approached him.

When it was all over, I went to Fauconberg and saw my love. But there was so much anxiety and pain between us that all did not go well with us. I wrote in my journal about the end of Jupiter.

"Never did I see such a barbarous execution, nor did it enter my thought that human nature could behave with so much spirit and resolution. I call it heroism in its way. Tied on the cross, his hand was chopped off, and with a large crowbar all his bones were smashed to splinters without him letting his voice be heard. Receiving at least four strokes on his left leg, and his arms not having been well tied, he raised himself on his middle to see what was the matter. All done and the ropes slacked, he writhed himself off the cross. Seeing the magistrates and others going off, he groaned three or four times and complained in a clear voice that he was not yet dead, not having expected he was going to be left in this condition. He begged the hangman to finish him off, but to no avail. He then sang and spoke with the people concerning the injustices of slavery, relating every particular with uncommon tranquility.

"But," said he abruptly, "by the sun it must be eight o'clock and by any longer discourse I should be sorry to be the cause of you losing your breakfast." Then casting his eye on a Jew whose name was De Vries, "Apropos, sir," said he, "won't you please to pay me the ten shillings you owe me?"

"For what to do?" asked De Vries.

"To buy meat and drink, to be sure—don't you perceive I am to be kept alive? Give me a pipe of tobacco."

This was met by hootings and curses. Next observing the soldier who stood sentinel over him occasionally biting on a piece of dry bread, he asked him how it came to pass that he, a white man, should have not meat to eat along with it.

"Because I am not so rich," answered the soldier.

"Then I will make you a present, sir," said the African. "First pick clean to the bones my hand that was chopped off. Next begin to devour my body until you are glutted."

He joked with the mob, tormenting them with reproaches and calling them barbarous dogs who ought to be damned for their cruelty. He lived from six-thirty till eleven, when his head was chopped off. He had died. They never killed him.

I walked with Joanna round Fauconberg and noticed that the place was run down and that the new overseer was so demanding that bitterness was growing among the slaves. I could foresee a wholesale dispersal of the plantation, with new slaves being brought in to increase the production of sugar.

"Joanna," I pleaded. "Will you not come to Holland? Will you not? You will have me, and you will have Johnny and many more."

She shook her head. "Here I am among my own people, among family, among friends. I have no right to leave them to their suffering. My mother will grow old. Then whither will she wander? Abandoned to the woods to live a solitary life? Like a wild pig?"

We went later to dine with Mrs. Godefrooy, to whom Joanna was pledged. But if I could find a way to purchase her outright, what then? I must have cut a very anxious and troubled figure that night. So burdened with evidence of terror I was, I could not do justice to the ample fare or entertain the company on my fiddle in my usual style.

"Oh, fie, good Stedman, what bothers you so? It is most affecting to see you so troubled," said my benefactress.

I recounted my anxieties about my dear Joanna. Here in Mrs. Godefrooy's presence alone, there was trust and I could talk of a love between two of God's creatures. She alone could understand that between mine and Joanna's hearts, wedged apart by the society, lay the desire to be together forever. I could confess to her the times I had been forced into liaisons with women who sought only to challenge my feelings for Joanna.

She said, "I know, good Stedman, of your manly sensibility for that deserving young woman and her child, and so much has this action recommended you to my attention that I shall think myself guilty if I do not participate in your laudable intentions. Permit me to offer you Joanna's full price of purchase this day, and you immediately redeem her in full. I hear conditions are unhappy at Fauconberg. Redeem beauty from oppression, tyranny, and insult." She placed all in writing in a trice.

I could not speak, but returned to Fauconberg with the money in my hat. De Graav, who was the director, received it with as much joy as I paid it and then gave me the portion he would have received in commission as a tangible appreciation of his pleasure at my purchase of my true love. Surely now she would follow me to the ends of the earth as my wife. After all that happened, and all that was known, she would not now spurn me in the eyes of my friends!

120

We paid Mrs. Godefrooy two hundred florins, and my account now lay at eighteen hundred florins, which would be no great amount to pay, counting on my industry and my drawing. Joy gushed out of me like water from a well. I danced with Johnny, gave Joanna a copy of the paper to free her, and took her to see the house which would be renovated for her in the orange garden at Godefrooy's, all the while hoping that she would reject it and follow me. In a week or two she would be free to occupy it with our son, as that good woman had become by virtue of the debt her protector. Now that Johnny's freedom was formalized he would have to be christened. (He had been "named" at Fauconberg on the ninth day of his birth. Cery had brought him out into the sunshine after his wine and water bath, and the old man had touched the infant's lips with water, salt, and yam flour and had spoken his name, "Robert Stedman," before the assemblage of well-wishers.) As I considered all the events of the past few days, Joanna's fears that our son would be sold to a Demerara River plantation receded. For the first time I was able to lie beside her in love without the ghosts of slavery beclouding our hearts. It was only then that I realized the barrier to our feelings that slavery had been.

The rebels had once more killed our soldiers, and by a most ingenious method. They had encircled a group of men and had forced them to retreat and fall into a snake pit. But this time they had also hurled gourds containing snakes into a place where some of our rangers lay sleeping. Many were bitten before they could imagine what was in progress. This was the type of warfare most feared by the men: the subtle poisoning of animals, which, though appearing well enough to walk, would be deadly when cooked and eaten; the poisoned water, corn, rice, and yams. The rebels sometimes abandoned old women and old men who, pretending to give information, would deceive us. The children saw us as devils and would rather drown themselves than be touched by us. Sometimes they left us the drink they brewed called "Kill Devil"; the soldiers, falling upon this spirit to ease their tribulations, were rendered even more wretched by it. The rebels knew the subtlest distinctions between what was good and what debilitated the constitution of white men.

Later, news came that the rebels had sunk a ship in their search for ammunition, and had taken some white people, including a woman and her child. It meant more patrolling of the plantations to ascertain where the white people were being held. It was very dry and hot in the woods. We marched to Cofaay, but we were unable to find any water. Instead, we found an old vegetable garden and destroyed whatever was good there.

Suddenly an old, tall Bush Negro appeared, wearing a white blanket. He approached the sentry and stood still. Giving him the talk, I invited him into the camp. He was an old man who had been abandoned by the younger group, but he shook his head and said, "No." Jumping into the bush, he disappeared. Two men angrily fired at him, but both missed. We made camp there and early next day took the path to Barbacoeba.

It was so dry that the fish were dying in the quagmire the Africans called a *biree-biree*. We came out of the woods at a plantation where a letter from Joanna reached me; that day my little son was two years old. With Quaco I drank to his health using all the wine I had and so was unable to celebrate St. Andrew's Day three days later by treating all the officers and men of the Scots Brigade to a glass of wine.

Without warning the weather changed; and it started to rain. Day and night, water gushed down upon us. There were no shelters for us, and sleeping outdoors had become like sleeping in a pool of water. One of our rangers was struck by lightning; his compatriots left him in the undergrowth to the mercy of the ants, crows, and *pingoes** because the lightning had declared him a witch. Nothing I could say would persuade slaves, soldiers, or rangers to touch him.

Another letter arrived from Joanna and with it some fruit and coffee, but I was so busy trying to construct a shelter that both got flooded away. I had never realized how difficult was the task of making a dwelling, which the Africans did with such ease. It was no effort for us to destroy the African dwellings and devastate their harvest of rice and corn, but I realized that it was the act of doing which made one man respect the labor of another.

A few days later we met up with Fourgeoud and another palaver took place between him and some rebels we encountered. I acted as his interpreter across the wide expanse of space that separated us, both sides agreeing to keep out of range of gunfire.

Fourgeoud: "You have deserted your masters because you are too lazy to work. You black rascals!"

Rebel General: "Hah! You stupid Frenchman. You run away your country, you too lazy to work! You stink. We smell you before we smell the *pingoes*."

Fourgeoud: "I am sure you are hungry. I promise you a good life: freedom, better food, and much rum to drink. Just lay down your guns."

Rebel General: "We are not hungry. You come see us. We give you full belly. We sorry for you—you stupid

---

*Wild pigs.

to kill for one bit* a day. White slaves! Scarecrows! Men with straw bellies! Where would you be without your guns? Bonny will be governor!"

After this they tinkled their bill hooks, fired a volley and gave three cheers for Africa. Then they dispersed to rest until we started hounding them again the next day.

Our men, sick with the bloody flux, had begun to desert, only to lose their way and die in the forest. While we coped with this trouble the rebels struck again, but we could not counterattack.

The slaves who had been carrying the ammunition with nothing to eat were so weak they had to be returned to their plantations. Not only were we starving, but our clothes were in shreds, our shoes rotted away, and our stockings eaten by the hungry insects of the wild. Once more Mrs. Godefrooy came to the rescue, and a third barge of food arrived. But in spite of it everyone was bad-tempered and cruel to the new batch of slaves, some being beaten for not picking up their loads and then again for picking them up too soon.

I had to decide in which direction to march. I foolishly went out into the forest and wandered away from the troops, and after trying to get back to them I realized I had lost myself in the wilderness. The more I tried to find my bearings, the deeper into the woods I seemed to go. I abandoned myself to despair. I began to think of my Joanna, my son, and life as a mass of unseparated feelings, experiences, and things. I discovered I was not alone; Quaco was beside me, fearful of the ghosts who inhabit the forests and the streams.

---

*Small colonial silver coin valued at eight cents in Guiana.

"Masera," he sobbed. "We deade! We deade!"

Round and round we went, fearful of stepping upon the venomous creatures that surrounded us. We encountered some monkeys called quata monkeys that threw sticks and excrement at us. Then Quaco put me in mind that on the south side the bark of the tree is always smooth. So by examining the trees we went south in silence. We heard coughing. *Mercy,* I thought, *what would the rebels do to us?* But we found troops resting near an old encampment. They had found safe, clean water, and I enjoyed the first cup of tea for many days. Quaco, who was faint, had a small calabash of grog, which revived him considerably.

My commander, Colonel Fourgeoud, after two weeks of marching, had reached Wana Creek, but I followed Colonel Seyburg, the commander of a battalion, to where Bonny had been seen. We missed him, and the walk was useless. This, I was told by Seyburg, had occurred because I had been stubborn in not getting there to order, and I was imprisoned and disarmed. My men threatened a rebellion, and in spite of my anger at their behavior and military disobedience, they actually protested my innocence. The rebels had gone back to pillage the Schoonhove and Altona plantations after news of Jupiter's death had perhaps reached them. There was no time for dissension among ourselves. I insisted that Colonel Seyburg and not I had been at fault and that I would, because I venerated truth, pursue the matter of blame to the bitter end.

Hearing that, Seyberg grasped my hand, begged me to be pacified, and declared that he would make peace on any terms. I insisted, however, that he own his fault in the presence of officers and erase from his journal every sentence that could reflect badly upon my character. This he did immediately and returned my arms to me; that settled the matter to my full satisfaction.

Even with men who should know better, my marriage to a slave girl sometimes was used against me. Many times they excepted me from invitations, drinks, and conversations, and some sought opportunity to sully and stain my character, as was the case in that instance. The last place to look for the rebels was at Gado Saby, or God Knows.

During our march to Gado Saby, Colonel Fourgeoud and I had discovered empty houses and a skull fixed to a tree, which we justly thought to be that of Officer Schmidt, who had newly come to us and in his ardor to kill got lost in the woods. While we were at Gado Sady we buried several men. The name meant "God knows," and it did the place justice.

One of the houses belonged to Bonny. It was set on stilts and had two doors, the better to observe all around him and to eliminate attack by surprise. Because it was so high aboveground the air circulated freely and sustained his health. Bonny had lately received a dangerous wound near the groin and walked with difficulty.

We found a wounded African left for dead under some manicole leaves. The colonel had insisted that he be taken with us, but the carriers saw him as a burden, handled him with little care, and subsequently abandoned him to a lonely death. But he had not died when I, bringing up the rear, came upon him, so we once more took him with us to Cofaay. It was a fertile place, well stocked with vegetables and nuts of all descriptions, which we began to burn. The flames got out of hand and overpowered our camp. The poor dying man had been left in the camp, now a mass of flames. It was hopeless to try to save him without destroying myself. There was nothing to be done.

My foot had started to swell again, and once more I could hardly walk. The surgeon reported me unfit for duty, and I lay in my hammock thinking of Joanna—of the first time I saw her, her sweet fifteen-year-old innocence, her intelligence and her accomplishments—and wondering why such a word as *slave* was ever invented. I thought of little Johnny, too—we had to stop calling him Jack when he demanded to have the same name as his papa. Amongst these thoughts Federicy's party returned with a captured African woman and her son. She had been taken years before by rebels, and her son, now eight, had been born in captivity.

We asked her about Bonny.

"He is very strict," she said, "and kills people for anything at any time. He kills people if they say good things about white men. Growing rice was the women's work, and the ricefields were our children. Don't burn the children!" she pleaded. "Take the rice for others to eat!"

My foot healed well from the attention given it by this useful woman; after it was cured, I found that I had two ulcers on my arms.

What pained me more, however, was my anger with Joanna. Did she no longer love me? Why wouldn't she write to me? I wrote a long, unhappy letter to her and also to Colonel Fourgeoud, who had left the camp and gone to Surinam, asking to be sent to the hospital at Devil's Harwar. Instead, I was sent to L'Esperance, and no sooner had I got there than she came. Our house was in a pitiful state, and so we went on to Facounberg to join my wife's family.

She had not yet taken possession of her house at Mrs. Godefrooy's but when we grew tired of the bustle of Fauconberg we went once more to our rented house in Surinam where I grew rapidly well.

But I was weary of a life always so close to death, such a restless unsettled life, and I fell upon my naked knees invoking heaven to lead me away from the service to which I was fettered by conventions and loyalties.

Some time later an annoying letter arrived from my mother. She made sure I knew of my brother Willie's successes, his delightful family, and his happiness. "Willie is always going forward," she said, "and him the younger son! You have your father's blood. I am strongly looking for a good wife for you. And this Joanna, why has she such a hold on you? Are you going to be a soldier forever?"

I suppose she meant well, so I wrote back telling her that something would happen soon. Joanna and I went on to Paramaribo, and we lodged with De Graav in his fine mansion. Colonel Fourgeoud had arrived there as well. He had regained his health and was most agreeable in his manners. He told me how well regarded I was by all who knew me, but I decided that I would step cautiously toward his friendship.

I was well enough to visit friends again and attended an evening of music and dancing with the black Mrs. Elizabeth (Zubbly) Sampson. It was a very genteel affair where the most up-to-date pieces of young Mr. Mozart were played. Joanna for the first time sang "Sidney's Just Exchange," which I often sang to her and played on my violin:

> "My true love hath my heart, and I have his,
> By just exchange one for another given

I hold his dear, and mine he cannot miss
That never was a better bargain driven.
My true love hath my heart and I have his,
My heart in me keeps him and me in one.
My heart in him his thoughts and senses guides
He loves my heart, for once it was his own
I cherish his because in me it bides
My true love hath my heart, and I have his."

The applause was rapturous. Joanna had begun to feel her freedom. She was no longer a slave and was well surrounded, schooled, and soon to be christened. She was such a beautiful woman and had been made more so by motherhood!

Yet she was afraid of the world and would be enfeebled by anything that was more demanding than the life she had always known. Mrs. Godefrooy had bought her beautiful dresses, and her daughter, Hetty, eager for a sister, had given her more. There were men of all kinds at the *convasione* (drawing room entertainment), and they looked at her with longing and even with resentment. There was an easy friendship between us, and I could feel my love for her sharp-edged and certain. But what was the point of it if it could go no farther than her native homeland?

A letter arrived from Henry, Joanna's brother, who was living in Holland. He felt homesick and would choose to come home. He was envied as Mr. De Graav's personal attendant, he said, and had been threatened by older servants within the household. Mrs. De Graav and her children loved him also, and that made matters worse.

We had replied, Joanna and I, with words of consolation and promised that he might yet see us in Amsterdam. But he wrote no more. He was now happy in his work, and we presumed that he had accustomed himself to the new work and the new place. I recalled the expectancy in his handsome face and the sense of adventure in his eyes when I accompanied him and De Graav to the town of Bram's Point on their way to Holland. Cery worried a little about her son, but Mrs. De Graav came to the plantation and assured her that all was well and she passed from La Bonheur, De Graav's plantation, to Fauconberg, which was the plantation of her enslavement.

I returned to Surinam from my patrol of Alkmar where I had gone to draw that place. I was going to patrol the river, I hoped for the last time. It had turned out that Moroccan pirates and not rebels had captured the whites from the sunken boat, and had taken them off to be slaves. We were all very sad as to the fate of the three men and one boy. The pirates had murdered a mixed-race boy and a soldier and left them on the beach for the crows to feast upon. Nothing could be done and they were simply taken up and buried. The most common death in this colony was death from beating, from mosquitoes, from diseases, and from murder, though for murder a small fine might be charged.

The slaves fought back with their spells and their poisons, and it was not unusual to hear of whole families being poisoned for cruelty to their slaves. Death came easily. It came as easily as life.

I had learned to love the black people. I had come to know their kindness, their loyalty, and their humanity and could not understand why they were treated in such an unchristian way by those who claimed an enlightened life as their heritage.

Part Three

The Sea Change

Seven

In company with Capt. Andrew Bolls, my second in command, and a couple of Africans, I decided to visit Goed Accord, which was the last sugar plantation on the Comewine River and the most accessible to the rebels, who were keen on enticing male slaves from their work to be soldiers and female slaves to become rebel "wives."

This was easy where there was cruelty on a plantation, but at Goed Accord the planter, Mr. Lange, as a matter of self-interest treated his slaves in a humane and indulgent way and in keeping with the name of his plantation. There was no need for whippings or the use of the *spambock*. This was an extremely severe punishment in which the slave was trussed up like a fowl and beaten first on one side and then on the other of his breach until his flesh was cut away. Slaves feared this flagellation, in which their wounds were washed with lemon juice and gunpowder to prevent mortification.

But the slaves of Goed Accord were free of all such punishments. The mothers and matrons held sway over the young. They smoked their clay pipes while seeing that everyone else earned their cornbread or *braf** or *tom-tom*† or *fufu,* which was made from pounded cooked plantains. The men often sat around talking or eating their *sweety muffo,*‡ which was made from the leaves of

*A hodge-podge of vegetables and meat.
†A pudding made of maize flour.
‡Sweet mouth.

tobacco chopped into pieces that could be chewed in comfort. As they chewed they talked, using the language of signs, which rebels also used when they hunted us in silence in the bush.

We were invited to dine at Goed Accord and served most surprisingly by tall, slim young women slaves, graceful and obliging in all service, but naked as the day they came into the world. This was an entirely unusual occurrence, and I inquired of my host why the nudity of the slaves had reached the dining table.

"It is their mothers and matrons who have forbidden clothing. They say that too-early intercourse and frivolous play with the men ruin the health and spoil the physical beauty of this particular caste from the Senegal," said Mr. Lange.

"The girls," added his wife, "are supervised for their virginity and, being of the Muhammadan persuasion, lose it at their peril. The matrons decide on husbands, and the girls must live in harmony with whomever has been chosen for them! All our slaves are pure stock."

I could see that Mr. Bolls was fairly gasping with the desire to touch these shapely, straight-limbed sable bodies, so smooth and rippling in their excellence, but when told that the permission of several dozen matrons must be individually obtained, his desires soon ebbed away. I was content to draw them, their legs, arms and fingers straight and finely shaped, their toes well splayed from generations of walking in the desert lands from which they had been taken.

When Mr. Lange, the plantation owner, made the decision to sell his slaves, buyers flooded in from all the plantations and much thought was given to the buyer whose bid would be accepted.

The rain was falling slightly when we left Goed Accord in a small barge rowed by two Africans. Soon, however, the drizzle became a downpour, changing the color of the river and bringing boulders toward us. Trees that had been brought down caused the barge to hesitate, to run against the tree trunks so that we jolted ourselves enough to be hurt and to allow our possessions to be washed away. My box containing my pencils and drawings catapulted into the river, but was retrieved by the alacrity of one of the Africans.

We reached Magdenburg late in the evening to find that Fourgeoud had already arrived there. With him had come new men and bearers. Fortunately, Quaco had been left to prepare my food, and that prevented the new men from taking over my hut with the door of entry in the roof, a trick which I had learnt from the rebels.

After the shocking black clouds of the rainstorm, the next day appeared scrubbed to a clean, clear crispness. My men and I began to march early to the northeast, and upon entering a swamp of formidable size, we started wading toward the opposite shore, where the trackers had seen rebels among the trees. We did not know what to expect, so dark and secretive was that place. We crawled silently among the green, knowing that the slightest crack of a twig or branch would betray us. We stopped dead before an open green space when a horrendous and daunting spectacle met our gaze. The ground was covered with fresh human remains, arms, legs, heads all carelessly thrown, while vultures sat waiting in the tall, close trees above us. Flies and ants, butterflies, beetles, and wasps were already busy about the charnel house in the green.

Hastily we buried the bodies and praised the bravery and the heroism of the men who had fallen there. Several individual parties had been sent out to scout, but when Captain Meyland's head, with his bright red hair and deep blue eyes, was found, we knew that it was his party that had been annihilated.

Several of the men had been so deeply moved that they were stopped from fleeing only by the treacherous terrain in which we had found ourselves located. And then, as if to bind us once more to our senses, we heard voices, almost sepulchral in the silence. A small party of rebels carrying baskets made of palm leaves upon their backs, and probably transporting rice, could be seen shadowy against the verdure. We started creeping through a narrow path and came upon a ricefield in the form of a square.

Adjoining the field but set at a distance from it were houses sheltered by lofty trees. The party of rebels appeared to have melted into the earth. There was a silence about us, expansive as the sky and deep as the ocean. We crept on, hardly daring to breathe. And then from the thickest part of the jungle the rebels in strict formation, as we could judge from the direction of the shots, began to fire upon us, mercilessly killing our men with a surprising accuracy of aim.

It struck me then that we were defending nothing and that our men were scared—much too scared to be soldiers. To many of our troops, life had become an illusion. They died without complaint. They died daily and were buried where they fell. But the rebels were defending their homes and themselves from the injustices of slavery and showed the fire of resistance by their deeds. They fought us with vigor and with skill, but as we were better-armed, they started to retreat across the barriers they had erected to thwart our progress.

We retaliated by setting fire to their fields, once more "killing their children," burning their huts and in the process recovering the property that had been pillaged from the plantations. The conflagration raged around us, the heat of the fire blending with the heat of the sun to overwhelm us. We retreated from the heat and at last sat exhausted among the debris and the dead, some of the men weeping, others unable to utter a sound. The smoke from the fires rose fitfully in the distance. The bracken crackled under the flames. But in my ears still echoed the shouts, the firing and swearing of soldier and rebel, the groans of the wounded and the dying, the shrill crescendo of the African horns, the prattle of their drums, and, in my mouth, the suffocating taste of the smoke.

Once more we buried the dead, saying the Lord's Prayer over all of them, rebels and soldiers alike. Some of our troops objected to the communal interment of the dead. I pointed out that they were dead and no one would know who was who when the ants had been. But they insisted on burying our dead and leaving dead slaves to the crows. While all this was taking place the rebels attacked us again. This time they used poisoned arrows and blowpipes as they attacked. They seemed to come recklessly close, yet our men were only slightly wounded. Then we saw that the rebels had loaded flints and shards of empty spa-water cans into their guns, so short of ammunition were they.

At about three o'clock we found a little bridge, rather like a hammock, suspended between two trees to provide a safe link across the rebel swamp, and so, mustering a small group of volunteers, I decided to pursue the rebels. We came upon more dwellings and ricefields and saw that the rebels had sent their women and children on ahead before the attack and that the shouting was to alert them as to the progress of the battle. Again we torched their fields and their dwellings. Around a three-mile radius we did not leave a blade of grass standing. There was utter desolation, and we were sure that the rebels could not survive there and must cross the river into the town of Cayenne in French Guiana, where the Dutch dared not go.

By nightfall my foot had once more become swollen to a considerable size and I had to be carried by two bearers, which was much against my disposition. It took us several hours to reach our camp, but the physician was immediately awakened to visit my foot and feared that it might have to be amputated. Fourgeoud, in a frivolous manner, said, "The Africans lose legs for kicking us, and now you are to lose yours for loving them."

I was ready to die of vexation, but contented myself by thinking of him as a Swiss-French lunatic. The next day I was taken in a tent barge rowed by eight men to Paramaribo. Quaco informed me that Mr. Renard, one of our surgeons, had been buried. He had died of a dreadful disease which first appeared with bilious vomiting and a yellowish cast of the countenance of the eyes. He died after just a few days of illness.

I found that Joanna seemed to be too reliant on Johnny being always with her. He called out, "Papa! Papa!" as I did to my own dear father, and she silenced him. I told Joanna that as soon as I was better I would have Johnny christened.

"What does it mean?" he asked. He began to cry.

"Don't be so timid," I said. "You will be made a Christian! A child of God, able to obey God's commandments."

Joanna shrugged, but as usual kept her thoughts to herself, although I could see scepticism written all over her face.

It started to rain, at first coming down in drops the size of stones and then in a wash and a rush. Johnny, unable to play, fell asleep where he had been sitting. He was a handsome child—like me, mainly, except for the tint of warmth in his skin.

"He would still be a quadroon," Joanna said suddenly. "One part of African blood is superior to three of white. It is the only time that black rises above white." She chuckled softly to herself, then continued. "I pray there is not so much cruelty, meanness, and hatred inside him." She looked at me as if expecting to find answers to all her fears in my face.

There was a rumble of thunder, and whips of lightning lashed the sulky gray clouds. The old pain ran through my foot like prongs of fire. The darkness, here in the hut at Hope was almost tangible; it made me feel suddenly alone and unhappy, and I recalled our cottage at L'Esperance that had been neglected so badly. Recollections stirred Joanna, too, for she sat beside me and stroked my hair. I felt the futility of the fighting, the deaths, the burning of the crops, and the certainty of starvation for the rebels. And the planters who caused it all lay in comfortable beds with their favorite slaves! "Oh, God," I sobbed. "Oh, God, help us all."

It was almost a mystery how rapidly the weather changed and all signs of what had been had vanished. A tent barge had brought the mail, and I received a letter from my mother. In spite of the caution which rippled through me, I opened and read it:

139

My son John,

Remember our next door neighbor Pieter Vonk?

The poor man is dead. I had paid him what you owed him for losing to him at cards, so you are free of debt to his estate. Willie's wife is soon to be in childbed, but you are in the bush with your blacks. The linnet I had for these twelve years died also, the cause being that it perched upon the chair from which I had just arisen. Not knowing it was there, I sat down once more—this time upon the poor bird, which caused me much unhappiness.

You have not yet sent me a recent drawing of your child. Do so soon to give me some knowledge of him. Will he always be a slave child?

My love to you, my son.

With affection
Mama

I imagined her bald consternation when she realized what she had done to her pet, but I sent her fifty florins to get another. Her letter pushed me into greater effort on Johnny's behalf. Would he always be a slave child whose name could never be mentioned? So being still unable to walk, I wrote to His Excellency pledging my word of honor (being all that I had apart from my pay) that should my son be made free of the degradation of slavery he would never become a charge upon the colony of Surinam. Quaco conveyed the letter, and I then sat down to wait the eternity when a reply would come. Joanna returned with Johnny to Fauconberg, leaving Sara, the Indian, to tend me. She said that the fever which made me shiver each night should receive treatment from Graman Quacey. My ankle was now healed, but I could only wear slippers. I spent my days reading and writing poems and reading over old letters while waiting for more to arrive. Henry, Joanna's brother, wrote from Holland, as he had been very fond of me and possessed much knowledge of birds, which was a sport of his. He said that the slaves resented his being set above them and were neither accepting nor friendly toward him. I replied in as consoling a manner as I could which greatly pleased Joanna, who came to bring me fruit from her plantation. She urged me to take the air using some crutches she had obtained, with Quaco to tend me.

But His Excellency that day sent his carriage for me, and after receiving me, he shook me by the hand and presented me with a letter proclaiming my son's emancipation forever. Imagine my feelings at being thus rewarded for my services to Surinam. Every hardship, every moment of searing thirst, every plague of bush and tree had been worth it. I hastened home to Joanna and she with the good news to Mrs. Godefrooy, who had come to town. My Johnny was now no longer a child of slavery.

There was nothing now to stand in the way of his christening, so with only my cane and my friend Captain Small, a good Christian man, for company, we went to wait upon the Reverend Snyderhaus to christen my son. To my great surprise he peremptorily refused even to consider such a task, alleging that, should I leave for Holland, I could not answer for my son's Christian education. Slowly, and deliberately controlling my temper so as not to further antagonize him, I explained that my son had two excellent guardians who would supervise not only his Christian education but his morals as well. It was all to no purpose. I remonstrated, persisted, and argued, but being the blacksmith's ecclesiastical child, he was as deaf to reason as his father's anvil and as empty of good sense as his father's bellows. In a fit of vexation

I told him I would rather see my son die a heathen than be christened by a bigoted and impudent fanatic.

"He must be foiled," said Small. "He must be foiled! Such types must never fly as eagles on the side of bigotry."

But we found the parsons to be a clique, each anxious to sit well at the other's table.

The troops had come out of the forest after Fourgeoud proclaimed that he had routed the rebels in all directions. He was for some the hero of the moment, but for others he was the object of contentious criticism and vilification. He had been accused of wasting money on an indifferent campaign. The rebels had not been vanquished, some said, only quelled—fleeing across a narrow river to return another day. Others accused Fourgeoud of paying us in paper money in order to keep the 10 percent that was lost to us. Others said that he had, with the connivance of Jews, sold the gold and silver recovered in the campaign, since we were not allowed to ask about the booty and no account was ever taken of it.

The last troops had been brought in from the Casepcore Creek, and the mere sight of them caused me to lay aside my cane and walk unaided. Bolls and I had just inspected the men and were remarking upon the dire predicament of some when chance led us past the courthouse. A crowd had gathered, mostly of mixed-race people—Joanna among them with Johnny. Imagine my consternation to see Jettee La Marre, the daughter of my late friend being brought to court in chains. She had returned home after her father's death and found herself a slave. She wept most bitterly, and when I intervened to mount a rescue she shook her head, saying, "There is

142

nothing you can do, sir. Nothing. This man demanded my maidenhead. My refusal has hurt and sullied his pride."

She was going to be tried by her mother's master, Mr. Van Schouten, for refusing to do the "task of a common slave." She was fourteen, had been christened and educated as a young lady, and had refused the attention of that lecherous old man with the box of curiosities. He had brought her to court so that the magistrates could confirm a private whipping. Happily, Mr. Wickens, the magistrate, was known to me and I was able to plead for leniency. He explained that she was in Van Schouten's power and must abide by his decrees. Fie! for her christening and her education!

I was so shaken that once more I begged Joanna for the sake of her security to leave injustice behind.

"This is what I know," she said in reply. "I would be melancholy without my people. And what if my mama dies or my grandpa? Who will Johnny have for relatives? Your mother regrets us."

"Zubbly Sampson has lived abroad," I countered. "Ask her what it is like. Let her tell you."

"She did tell me," said Joanna. "You must belong to the abolitionists, or you are ill regarded. She was laughed at, followed, and pointed out. *She* had been baptized!"

"Johnny will be," I said. "Lay aside vexation."

"Vexation or not," she said, "I do not hold control of the matter."

We walked home silently, knowing full well what was meant by the "task of a common slave" and that baptism carried no favors or recognition by those whose institution it was.

Later that evening the officers and men were invited to dine with Colonel Fourgeoud. And though I felt aggrieved, I decided to attend. There were only four of us, and he served us roast beef sent from Holland in a sealed tin with newly picked potatoes, vegetables, and gravy. He thanked us individually for our help with an expedition that had been punishing, demeaning, and dishonorable. I complimented his skill in command and gave him drawings of himself and of the camp at Magdenburg. In the midst of it I began to shake with fever, one minute hot, another cold. He also advised me to seek treatment from Graman Quacey, whose cure for this fever was well known.

Joanna and I went to call upon Graman Quacey at his elaborate home, where he kept slaves of his own. He showed me his fine furniture and silver plate. He then offered me refreshments, which I declined, pleading the poor condition of my health. He examined my hair, the palms of my hands, the soles of my feet, and my eyes and then said that bugs, ticks, and mosquitoes had deposited poisons in my blood which he would sweat out of my system in his bath hut. He gave Joanna some bitter bark with which to brew me a drink for each of nine nights. He sat me in the bath hut on a seat and allowed his slaves to encircle me with hot stones on which cold water was poured. The heat emanating from the stones so affected me I was wet with sweat and almost faint with the desire to sleep. When at last I was taken out, I was laid down upon a couch, and there I slept for a full two hours and awoke feeling fresh and rejuvenated.

He sent us by his coach to Mrs. Godefrooy's where a dance was in progress. A galliard was being exquisitely performed in honor of that kind lady, in celebration of a visit to the Jews' Savannah of her ancestry.

She beckoned to us, and beside her sat the good reverend. I was just about to spurn him when she said, "Reverend Snyderhaus has offered to teach Johnny his catechism and baptize him, Stedman. Trouble yourself no longer."

I nodded stiffly in acknowledgment.

It was now official. We were leaving Surinam and were to be entertained at the colonel's headquarters. His headquarters, fie! It was not a place of any quality. It was cramped and plain, with an old stable lantern with broken glass teetering above our heads. He took the opportunity to recount his achievements against poor, ill-equipped people taken from their homes to work under the whip, and who opposed us with valor, ingenuity, and determination.

"Officially, the expedition has ended," he said. "And, considering the terrain, there has been little bloodshed. We never once underestimated the enemy, their skillful formations, and their knowledge of the bush. We have destroyed twenty-one towns or villages, demolished two hundred fields with vegetables of every kind, burned innumerable huts, and to date our spies have told us that the rebels have fled to Cayenne. I want to thank all those fighting men who risked life and limb and health against rebellion."

He was heartily congratulated and we drank his health as the savior of the colony. I was asked to reply. I praised him for never deliberately putting captive rebels to death and said that he was an indefatigable, brave, and undaunted officer. He then explained the arrangements that had been made for us to board ship and leave Surinam.

My feelings were sadly mixed. I paced the room one minute with feelings of despair and at another with relief for the company. But there was as yet much to be done.

I appointed Robert Gordon and James Gourlay, two friends who had fought and endured dire hardships with me, as guardians for my sweet child and Mrs. Godefrooy, his surrogate grandmother, as his godmother. With Joanna we watched as he was christened.

Joanna, who all along had kept control of herself, was now distracted with worry at my departure. She was dejected and silent, yet inflexible in her desire to remain in Surinam. In the end I accepted her choice. She had effectively sent me away. I felt rejected and hurt, for I had sincerely believed that she loved me, and never once had I been cruel or critical of her, and only on one or two minor occasions had I toyed with others when I slept at plantations. She I loved and would always love.

We sat a doleful pair, wrapped in our thoughts until Beatrice came to say their grandfather had that afternoon died. We hastened to Fauconberg and found the preparations for the burial well in progress. All the close male relatives had already shaved their heads and sat around with the other men chewing *sweety muffo*. The coffin had already been made, in this case, because he had many children to find the cost of it, from the best wood. As the time of the burial approached, he was laid in the coffin, his family sprinkling flowers over him and talking to him as though he were alive. They took leave of him, touching his brow and promising to see him once more in the land of the ancestors.

They laid him in a grave dug on this plantation, in the slaves' cemetery, and then completely filled in the grave. After covering it over with turf, they placed a gourd of water and another containing his favorite food upon it. Then, because he had been a mason, they put a large brick beside the gourd. He had chosen many wives, never letting himself get bored with any of them, and had begotten in excess of twenty children. By now the feast was well in progress, and at this feast bonds of friendship between the living were strengthened in dancing, halloing, singing, clapping, and the sound of the drums.

The next day I returned to Mrs. Godefrooy's, where I received a message that our orders to sail had come. Quaco hastened to fetch Joanna, and she arrived in a state of grief and turmoil. Weeping, she begged me to stay, since she could not dispose of herself. Her family clung to me, all weeping that one whom they so dearly loved should leave them never more to return to them.

How I wished I could have purchased all their freedoms! I took a lock of Joanna's hair and of my dear Johnny's, and then, tearing myself away, I went to join my ship. But on being told that the orders had been changed, I was given some respite.

On board ship I entertained Gordon and Gourlay and was told that we would not be ready to sail for another two days. They encouraged me to stay on shore a little longer with dear Joanna and her boy. But alas! Too dear we paid for this too-short reprieve, since but few hours had elasped on shore when a sailor abruptly came in with the message that the ship's boat lay in waiting that minute to carry me on board that instant. Heavens! What were my feelings! Joanna's mother took the infant from her arms, the all-worthy Mrs. Godefrooy supporting Joanna. Her brothers and sisters hung around me, and Joanna, holding me by the hand, was unable to offer one word. I perceived she was distracted—the hour had come. I pressed them both fondly to my bosom. The power of speech also forsook me, and my heart tacitly invoked the protection of Providence to befriend them.

Joanna now shut her beauteous eyes. Her lips turned the pale color of death. She bowed her head and sank motionless in the arms of her adopted mother. Here I

roused all my remaining fortitude and, leaving them surrounded by every care and attention, departed and bid
God bless them. (From the Stedman journal, ed. Stanbury
Thompson, as published by the Mitre Press, Buenos Aires,
1962.)

Motionless and speechless, I hung over the ship's
stern until the colony of Surinam and all land had disappeared. But my Joanna came to me in the flashes of the
sunlight and in the glinting of the waves and in the stars
like tears in the sky that night. Not only had I loved her
but, because of her, I had grown the habit of viewing
Africans with an unjaundiced eye. I had seen the horrors
of slavery and could never understand why Europeans
sought to perpetuate it by a constant refinement of its
terrors. Of all the officers that had sailed out in 1772, I
was the only one returning. Had it not been for Joanna
I, too, would have been no more.

She possessed so many fine qualities, but was un-
aware of them. She was content to do as she was told,
surrounded by the women of her family and satisfied to
know that they were close. I suppose her family gave
her feelings of containment, so important because the
overwhelming power of slavery was its ability to leave
people feeling exposed. At any time a slave could be
killed, beaten, or mutilated, and no questions were ever
asked. Helplessness and vulnerability were the scars of
slavery.

As I thought these things, my need of her over-
whelmed me so that I retired to my hammock and wept.

Eight

We were at sea six weeks and had another six to go. Having passed the tropics, we were becalmed for some days. At about fifteen degrees north latitude we found the sea covered over with a floating green and yellow weed, very curious when dried and pressed between two sheets of paper. The weed resembled trees, flowers, and shrubs in which small crustaceans dwelt, such creatures as scallops and mussels and a small reptile, the hippocampus or sea horse. Once more, as on our way to Surinam, we were swamped by flying fish as they fell upon the decks, an indifferent look upon their faces. Several porpoises and grampuses tumbled before and after our ship as if delighted to escort us and keep us company.

Some of the crew had become violently seasick due to the rocking of the ship upon their constitutions, which were weakened by the life in the harsh climate of tropical Surinam and the commotions and trials of a proprietary guerrilla war in the unyielding forests. Some men had died and had already been buried at sea, to become part of its mystery and its abundance. The creatures that had made the sea their home, when procured for drawing by various means, never failed to dazzle my understanding of creation.

The weather glorious, the skies pale blue with smudges of indigo, the clouds free-flowing and clean—all this suddenly turned, causing heavy rain accompanied by lightning and thunder that continued throughout the night and brought the topsail down on us.

The men were too weak to move it away, but I cheerfully seized an axe and began cutting the mast loose as if I had been toiling once again at a manicole palm in the forest. The two days following, we continued scudding before the wind with a reef in the foresail and the sea mountainous and constantly breaking over the vessel, thus bringing all hands to the pumps.

We passed many craft bound for different parts of Holland. We saluted them, and after giving ourselves up to numerous halloos and cheers, we sailed on.

One morning we found a carnage among the animals on board—monkeys, baboons, fowl all pitifully mangled, some still in the throes of death. A violent argument ensued among the men as to its cause. Men who loved animals as God's creatures argued with those who hated them as bickering, fierce battles broke out and continued until nightfall. We then organized a rigid watch over the remaining animals. At dead of night, a sly outline appeared from the direction of Mr. Neysus' room. He was one of our surgeons and had a *crabbo daggo* (crab-dog) or *grison* for a pet; this savage animal, renowned for its blood lust, alacrity, and deadly bite, had been responsible for the carnage. It killed even when glutted; as long as there was life, it kept on till all was dead. The men, jumping out of their hammocks with sticks and billhooks, began to harry it.

"Spare my Arante [crab-dog]!" pleaded Mr. Neysus. "She meant no harm! 'Tis her nature."

By now her ferocity sparkled like fire in her eyes. The men had cornered her, teasing her and prodding her to take to the sea and swim to death, but she would not.

Eventually, as she dashed toward him, Mr. Neysus himself knocked out her brains with a hand pike. She was no larger than a domestic cat, yet killed and devoured quadrupeds many times larger than herself. Gowsary had said he had seen these animals hunting crabs among the mangroves of a Berbice creek in the early dawn.

For three days the ships had been running before a fine wind, until we found ourselves stuck fast upon a large, soft sandbank covered with shallow water outside Amsterdam. There we lay becalmed all night, and there we remained until the third day, when a fresh breeze sprung up and helped us clear.

I felt cold to the marrow of my bones, even when dressed in my greatcoat, and I marveled at the constitutions of the Norwegian passengers, who were enjoying the weather on deck in their shirts.

The men's spirits soared higher each day, but I thought constantly of Joanna and Johnny. Even among the troops of men who had shared my experience, I felt isolated and rejected. Why could she not follow her husband in the manner of most wives? Was it because Cery never saw her children as burdens upon her?

June of 1777 had arrived while we sailed; with its end also came our journey's end to Bois-Le-Duc in Holland, where the men would do duty at the garrison.

Six lighters were appointed to transport us to our destination, and many people had come out to welcome us; I was fascinated, not only by their numbers but by their appearance. After the sparkling eyes, ivory teeth, the smooth, sable, and mellow skins, and the remarkable cleanliness of the Africans, both slaves and freedmen, of Surinam, these people seemed an ill-formed, ill-dressed, pig-eyed rabble. I could hardly bear to look at them. I had completely forgotten that I was one of them and that they must have been astonished by our overtanned and sun-broiled appearances.

We passed before General Hardenbrook and eventually the troops were cleared and received their service pay packets. Although they had earned them like horses, they spent them like asses.

I now took my leave of Colonel Fourgeoud's Dutch regiment by requesting my resignation to coincide with my readmission to the Scottish regiment of General Stuart, who had previously been my commander.

His regiment had established a long and distinguished link with Holland, one that dated from the sixteenth century to the siege of Bergen op Zoom by the French in 1747. With my heart a well of joy, I readily laid aside the blue coat of the Dutch nation and donned the bright scarlet of my former regiment, and with Quaco in brilliant livery I set out, riding a fine chestnut horse, to rejoin my compatriots in Steenbergen, where I had first been garrisoned before the voyage to Surinam.

Delighted to see me again, General Stuart feted me and presented me to His Serene Highness the Stadtholder, who, for my services, promoted me to the rank of major. In acknowledgment of the honor I presented His Highness with eighteen wax figures of the free Indians and African slaves engaged in different occupations. Even a simple act like that flooded me with memories of Joanna. I had modeled myself as an African wearing a basket, and though I could not remember the number of baskets I had made for her, I clearly recalled the delight that shone like stars in her eyes when she had received them.

At this meeting also, I was offered the lieutenant-governorship of the colony of Berbice, where the slaves had rebelled so often. It was close to Surinam and not dissimilar in climate, and so I promised to think about the matter and visit the directors for further discussions. I recalled the soldiers I had met from Berbice—Baron, a rebel leader, Akur, Gowasary, Marquis, Philander, and Quashi who had been promised his freedom and who threw the children from the roof when his master reneged on that promise. They had all been intelligent and tenacious, if cruel, men—the cruelty, however, first having come from their masters.

With Quaco, I journeyed to the Hague. The directors, after congratulating me heartily, offered me the highest salary they had ever offered to any gentleman. But beyond that they could not go. It was not in their power to offer a pension after a certain number of years, and there would be no substantial fortune to leave behind for my heirs. Once more I recalled the perils of the climate and my years of sickness and suffering in Surinam. Once again I felt the rapier stings of the mosquitoes, the throbbing hole in my ankle, and my body racked with fever. Quietly I renounced the idea and decided to recover health and vigor in Europe.

At home in Breda I quickly became aware of the new political situation spawned by the war with the American colonists. In December of 1780 Holland declared war against Great Britain. With these two powers at war, the Scots Brigade regiments were practically interned by the Dutch. We spent our time exercising the troops, often twice a day, going on long marches, and, in our spare time, drinking, gaming, and wenching. There were deserters in a steady stream and beatings, and bastinading was common. It was on those days when boredom descended upon us that I began to regret my neglect of the opportunity to govern Berbice and begged an acquaintance's assistance in the reinstatement of the matter, as he had become influential in the Court of Policy where the governorships were decided.

I found myself passing time in the same old ways—an evening in the bawdy house, riotous drinking, sleeping each night in the rooms of different young ladies, and writing and receiving letters. I did not know what to write to Joanna, but I was delighted to receive a letter from her. I felt ashamed of myself, but for some reason I also felt unable to stop myself from the pursuit of carnal pleasures.

Dear John,

I send you greetings from Johnny and me and also from all the relatives at Fauconberg, which is in a sorry state of decay. I hope that your health is no longer a blight to your constitution. We miss you more as time passes, and we are all sure you will return to this place where there is so much deep and honest love for you. I have a little shop now where I sell coffee beans from the plantations.

Van Schouten is dead—shot by a man who, since he cannot be found, has been taken among the common folk to be Jettee in man's clothing. She was so damaged she was bed-bound for days after he had his way. I hope it was her. But it is all "a langa langa story." Henry finally died after being so sick for so long. He returned home to us from Holland in a sorry state. He wasted away and had surely been poisoned. Anyway, we took care of him and knew that the end would come.

I am sending you some sweetmeats for your entertainments. Will you come back to us? When will you come? Will you ever come, dear John? When I am low with the thought of slavery, you shine like a star in my heart. And Johnny—when he smiles, you smile, too. Thank you for paying yet more to Mrs. Godefrooy. It is but two hundred florins left. Will you ever come? We have sown your name in pepper cresses as you once did ours at Hope. As for Mrs. Godefrooy, all I can ever say is "Gado sa bresse dat woman."

Your affectionately, etc.

P.S. Jettee has visited me. We laughed and we cried. I now know who it was. She has such courage—that girl.

Joanna

This was so typical—so pleasant and yet so conceal-ing of her pain. When the organ plays Mozart on Sun-days, she comes to me. Whenever there is moonshine making shadows and gleaming upon the river, she comes to me. And when there is pleasant prospect in the dis-tance, she comes and with her our life at L'Esperance, the two of us sitting with our child among the chirruping birds and the flowers. But nowadays, with the hurly-burly of life, the pressures and the politics, needs must seek out thoughts of her. Cathy Glover, one of my most indulgent of mistresses, had come back into my life, grasping at my time, my manhood, and my need to forget with eager hands. I was as a winged seed in the wind without Joanna, wind-blown hither and thither.

I took refuge from lovers by living at home with my mama, but it was like going from the feast to the fair. Mama regarded me as her recalcitrant child again and talked constantly of marriage. I moved into my own house, where I could sit alone with my memories, which could be neither sullied nor taken from me. Sometimes I was content just to lie in bed reliving the mornings from long ago, with Johnny and Joanna beside me.

Cathy was embarrassed when I talked of my love for Joanna, as the word *slave* had only a pejorative meaning to her.

"How could you have loved a slave when there were so many beautiful white women?" she once asked.

"Slaves can be beautiful, can be women, and can be loved—I looked beyond the word," I explained. "There were no barriers to love. In my arms my Joanna was just a lovely woman."

I showed her pencil portraits of Joanna, and like me, Cathy was sad that such a woman could not bear to be parted from her people. I spent all night with Cathy in my arms and Joanna in my heart.

After Cathy had left, a thought came suddenly to me. In Johnny Joanna had me and would always have me. In him she and I would both survive. Love for her was a moment, and what came after was supportive of that moment, which was celebrated in her child. Her thoughts of motherhood, wifehood, and love had all been shaped in the institution of slavery, and what I had offered her was beyond her comprehension. She could not understand the inner workings, the bones, the blood, and the muscles of the life of a woman in freedom.

Slaves never knew, nor could they try to know, what their mistresses thought or felt other than the scorn, the anger, the spite, and the revulsion they showed their slaves. Joanna could never have understood the life of a woman without the supports of her tribe and her community, against which she would place the framework of her decisions. I would go back, I promised myself, to free my son, and a part of that freedom would be a new environment in which he would learn new functions and view new horizons. For him life would never be a series of moments as uncertain and frightening as nightmares from hell.

I did not reply to Joanna. Instead, I sent a poem titled "Lodge":

Love in my bosom like a bee
Doth suck his sweet.
Now with his wings he plays with me
Now with his feet.
Within my eyes, he makes his nest
His bed amidst my tender breast.
My kisses are his daily feast,
And yet he robs me of my rest,
Ah wanton will ye?

I safely enclosed it in a letter to Mrs. Godefrooy!

Dear Mrs. Godefrooy,

    It is four years since I left Surinam and I have accepted that Joanna does not desire to leave Cery and face change. I owe Joanna my life and have loved her to distraction, and when I think of my son no seas or oceans should divide us even if the voyage takes three months.

    I have discussed with you the depths of my affections for Joanna and the restrictions that the accursed institution of slavery imposed upon us. My rest is often sullied by the confusions in my heart, but life must go on. I remember and keep your birthday and hope that your life will be long and blessed. Recollections fade, and I must work my passage through life and do what I must. How I wish she would cross the line of change. I feel so helpless now and once again have given myself over to recklessness and instability.

Your affectionate friend,
Stedman

After six months Quaco arrived from Zutphen, a town in Holland where, waiting to receive my luggage,

am ready to pass over the rest of it if Joanna would but let me.

Van Schouten has been shot, and Jettee is free. Also, the Frenchman, Destrades, has been discovered to have been a thief. When shot by a pistol and his bleeding attended to, the mark V for voleur was revealed, a burn upon his shoulder. It was a sad exposure, because he strove hard to be regarded a gentleman.

The times have strangely changed since you left, good John, but my son, his family, and I enjoy God's blessings in good health, easy hearts, a good table, and peace and contentment here at Alkmar, our peaceful plantation. Miss Spaan has been poisoned. She killed a beautiful girl by pushing a hot poker into her body. Her private parts! Stedman! Dreadful! Are we traitors to our race when we say no to such evil?
Yours, etc.

E. Godefrooy

P.S. De Graav has spoken of what is to come. I regard her a lucky lady. Send us your news.

De Graav had innocently betrayed a confidence. Indeed, I had dined with him when he had come to Maestricht, a strongly fortified town with a handsome bridge across the river Meuse in Holland, and had introduced him to Adriana Wierts. He had remarked upon the wisdom of attachment to one but little over half my age. I had met her when, at Mama's invitation, she had come with her two older sisters to visit my pictures. She had been lively and intelligent, while her dull, stolid sisters peered from behind their heavy eyebrows and doll-like faces.

Her youth and freshness had released in me, as Joanna had done, the desire to nurture and protect. She understood what I tried to express in my paintings, and she was not afraid to join in my admiration of Joanna. She was young and free of guile, but was passionate and even hysterical. But that made me further want to protect her. She differed from Joanna in that she knew how to choose. Joanna had always been told what to do.

Mama was delighted that the youngest daughter of a family she respected and admired had succeeded where so many had failed. She wrote letters and busied herself until Quaco informed me that he was sure she had written to Joanna.

"Where is the letter?" I asked.

He did not know. Nor could he say what it had contained.

"Did you write to Joanna, Mama?" I asked her over dinner.

"Of course," she said. "I wanted news about the child." She never called him grandchild as far as I could recall. "After all, my blood is there and I want to know about the blood—contaminated or not."

"Exactly what did you say?"

" 'Would you please let me have some news of my grandson, John? I am an old woman and will see but a few more years. I would like to make the acquaintance of your son by your writing to me. Mrs. Stedman.' "

I did not know what to think. Quaco said she had laughed and joked to Mrs. Fielderman, the neighbor, about shocking "that slave girl" with her news. Each Sunday all those women went to church and hung out their sins to air, and then they replaced them on Monday. Each Sunday Adriana and her sisters and parents went to church, and during the week I returned to Cathy, Mitie, Suzie, and all the other girls I had met. The marriage with Adriana was slowly set, but it might never have taken place at all had not the peace been signed and I had to change my life. In a moment of abandonment to fate, I asked Adriana's hand. To escape her family, she readily accepted. She was a fine woman even when measured against Joanna.

She had come from a distinguished family of naval engineers, and I had met her father often. He was slightly my senior in age and had a number of sisters of marriageable age. The men of the regiment courted Wierts because of his many pretty sisters. He was a quiet, high-principled man who lived for his children, several of them by two wives—one dead and him yet with the other, my wife's stepmother.

After the peace was signed, the Scots Brigade was being repudiated by a Dutch government determined to destroy the brigade's connection with Britain. In 1782 the States General, which was set over all the states of Holland, adopted a resolution that the officers of the brigade must forthwith either swear an oath abjuring allegiance to the British crown or forfeit their commissions and quit the service of Holland.

Those of us who had wholeheartedly served the Dutch nation, risking life and limb in its cause, saw this offer of choice as lawless impudence. At once, sixty-one of us resigned our commissions and put into effect the preparations for our departure from the country.

I was in the depths of this activity when a letter arrived from Gourlay, Johnny's guardian. As soon as I received it there came over me the most intense feelings of dread. Something was surely amiss. My hands began to shake, my body to tremble, but I stilled myself and opened it.

161

Dear Stedman,

I send you sorry news. Since news of your marriage reached Joanna, she seemed to have gone awandering into a foreign world. On the fifth of November she was found dead. She had always hoped you would return. She was mocked and derided, and many envied her position.

It is a sad day for us all to lose a woman so incomparable and so beauteous. God give you the strength you need at this dark hour. I know what this news will mean to you. The boy is as well as can be expected, although he understands but little of the whole affair. Your marriage was her death knell. She smiled and yet did not. But death comes when it must. So free yourself from being the cause of it and look to the living.

Your obedient servant,
R. Gourlay

The news sounded in my head like a thousand anvils being beaten. I sat down, too stunned to talk and for days unable to move or even think. Adriana, whom I had married the previous February, had never seen me thus and did not know how to mend me. I sat alone night and day, thinking of Joanna, hearing her laughter, seeing her fingers scurrying along the keys of Jettee's spinet. I recalled, too, her good sense at wearing her worst dress to wait upon De Graav when he became the director of Fauconberg. I felt as if my heart had been wrung out. I wrote to Mrs. Godefrooy.

Dear Madam,

What did evil fools say to my Joanna? There was no need to rejoice because I was married after five years of waiting for her to change her resolutions. Oh, Joanna!

My love! My life! How can I accept that I was not the
cause of her death? Did she suffer? And what of my son?
Is he being comforted and consoled and loved? Please let
it be known that his father loves him doubly now.

Stedman

Time dragged while I waited to hear from Mrs. Godefrooy about what had really happened to dear, sweet Joanna. At last she wrote to me:

Dear John,

Joanna was never happier than the night before she
died. Contrary to belief your marriage resolved something
in her, and her coffee shop, which she had opened with
my help to sell coffee beans, was doing a good trade among
the troops who had newly come here and were enamored
of the drink. She had gone out with Beatrice to a wedding
party and came back unwell. The next day she was dead.
The doctor said she had been poisoned, and Sara, the Indian woman, said she had certainly been and that she
knew who had poisoned Joanna. Two days after that was
put about, two of my own house slaves had jumped into
the canal and drowned themselves.

I will ask Gourlay to convey Johnny to your care as
soon as the question of Joanna's estate has been settled.
She was a mere twenty-four years old, but so perfect was
she, it was a delight to open my eyes and see her first
each morning. God rest her soul. We buried her in the
orange grove she loved, among the trees and flowers.
There will be no peace for those who harmed her. My poor
old heart mourns the death of this blessed child, whom I
so dearly loved. God grant her eternal rest.

Your affectionately,
E. Godefrooy

163

The Christmas Day after Joanna's death was one of the saddest days in my life. Adriana came from a large family, and they celebrated Christmas with a great deal of ceremony. Pleading that my papers needed attention, I set aside all frivolity, turning to the Good Book for comfort. I asked God to free me from the guilt of causing the death of the one person I loved most in the world. Adriana had come into my life when I had reached riper years, but with Joanna I had played like a child in the fields, chasing, hallooing, and reading beautiful verse and finding love's essence. Now she was no more. God knoweth all and will grant her eternal peace.

Johnny came to us in the late summer of 1784. I remember the morning when Gourlay helped him into the lighter that would bring him ashore. He kept looking for me. When he had seen me he smiled and, cautiously as his mother would have done, came toward us and bowed, first to his new mama and his grandma and then to me. I could not contain myself. I hugged him. He was my son—a composite of past people and present. There was my father in the cut of his nose and Joanna in the shape of his mouth. He was tall and straight, with my blue eyes and just a touch of olive in his skin. His teeth were white and even, and when he smiled it was as if one had been struck by a blast of sunshine. His smile was like Willie's, slow and scanning yet sincere.

"Mama died," he said in Dutch. "They put her in a box and then into the ground. I poured milk over her because she was my mama and gave me milk. They buried her in the orange grove, and everybody wept. She told me all must one day die."

I wept as only sadness could—his words as barbs upon my heart. We went home to tea. And when we sat down, my grief fell away. I was whole again. I had all my family at one table. And in Johnny I had Joanna, too. Gourlay had brought Johnny's inheritance, upward of two hundred pounds in a silver purse I had given Joanna.

"She was concerned with having two thousand florins," said Gourlay. "But she would never tell me the reason. Why?"

I knew why. "It was her worth in plantation money," I replied.

This good man had taken infinite care of my family and had brought my son to me. I therefore bade Johnny present one hundred florins to him.

I had become disillusioned with life and events in Europe and was determined to leave Maestricht, where I had lived as a youth before I went to Surinam and since my marriage in February of 1782. We set about taking leave of our friends. At the same time, I vowed to do my bit to disclose the horrors of slavery that I had witnessed with my eyes and with my heart. Johnny had seen it, too, and with Joanna's death I felt compelled to stand up for the injustice she had experienced. My attempts to free my son were greeted with derision from friends in Surinam, but a wider world existed and there I would speak. I asked Mr. Neysas to take a letter to Mrs. Godefrooy, as he was going home to Surinam.

Dear Mrs. Godefrooy,
    I am indeed grateful to you for sending my son to me so well and hale. He is an uncomplaining child and gives me great pleasure in his dealings with his new mama. We are going to England as the situation dictates, but you will always be remembered as a true and loving

165

friend. Thank you for mourning Joanna. I too mourned her, as I did my father, by wearing a black band on my arm and on my sword. Johnny will mourn fully. Pray God we make good of our situation, and believe me, my heart bleeds for my dear Joanna, whose life has been so short. I pray that she knew that I thought only to bring her happiness. I cannot and will not accept that she took poison when she so feared pain. That thought is hard to bear.

God bless you always,
Stedman

P.S. My wife and my son also invoke God's care upon you and your family. When as a boy of ten I returned from Scotland and my uncle's care, I was so thick with lice and dirt, I had to be cleansed with gunpowder and water. Thank you for the fine, clean boy who came to us.

We left Maestricht in a coach and six horses, pack and baggage, escorted by my brother and Lewis Black of the Dragoons. On the *Thosse* we sent back two horses after giving them a double feed. The first night we slept at S'rouge au bateau, a beautiful town, and then passed through the Austrian territories and found the annual fair in one town so crowded we could buy no food. At the Mop Fair we saw many hundreds of tradespeople standing in a long line and holding the tools of their trade for employment's sake.

In Brussels the people were preparing for a fifteenth-year jubilee. There was much noise and bustle, which greatly disturbed my dear in her delicate condition. We set off from there to Dunkirk. The roads were dreadful, especially when we went over the quicksands. The breakers beat into the carriage, and the horses were exhausted. My wife became more and more agitated, but by heaven's protection we arrived at Calais. We met some people called Anderson from Edinburgh, but my wife, being Dutch, limited their intercourse with us.

The St. Johns, a bigoted English couple we had met in a teahouse, refused us a passage in their packet, and after twelve hours in a French packet we arrived at ten o'clock in the evening at Dover. We were exceedingly hungry and the child tired, and we were shown to a garret at the York Hotel. Our goods were once more picked through and plundered, as they had been by the French customs, but we survived all and the next day set out in a post chaise for London. In Canterbury we secured excellent bed and board and also slept soundly in good, clean beds at the King's Head in the town of Rochester. It had been a long and tiring journey, but the end was now in sight as we set out in the post chaise for London.

For the past weeks our existence had been naught but fragments that all came together, and we arrived at Macaulay, my dear friend's door, No. 14 Princess Street, Hanover Square, at four o'clock. Here we dined most heartily and Johnny was soon sound asleep. I visited him to see if all was well, and there he lay, looking more like his mother than ever. It was as if she had suddenly come to remind me of her lost existence. I knelt down beside the bed, hoping to pray for guidance in the task of healing and helping him. I tried! Oh, how I tried! But all I could whisper was, "Joanna, oh, dear, dear Joanna."

I retraced my steps. The women had retired. Macaulay sat quietly smoking his pipe. We had been friends all my soldiering life.

"Are you enjoying some *sweety muffo*?" I asked him jocularly.

"Yes," he said. "Do join me."

The quiet pipe and the scent of the tobacco brought many people to my thoughts. I recalled David Douglas, who had been whipped to death; Gowasary, who was drowned at Magdenburg; Akera, who deserted and went back to Berbice; Quashi, who had killed three children; Jupiter, who had been broken on the rack; and Joanna's old grandfather, blinded by the masonry dust that had filled his eyes and his lungs throughout his long years of servitude.

"What are your thoughts about Surinam now?" asked Macaulay. "Now that you can take the long view?"

This time I answered in my own verse:

"Some Afric chief will rise who, scorning chains,
Racks, tortures, flames, excruciating pains,
Will lead his injured friends to bloody fight
And in the flooded carnage take delight,
Then dear repay us in some vengeful war
And give us blood for blood and scar for scar."

"Another puff of smoke. Another breath. Good night, Stedman. Good night. Have a good rest. You deserve it," Macaulay said.

Sleep had come upon us with such urgency we could no longer tarry. I slept the sleep of the just that night and woke to all the sounds of London. I rose and dressed while my wife, in her delicate condition, continued to lie abed. Johnny, upon hearing me about, joined me, and together we walked in Hyde Park. The dew was still as molten silver upon the grass, and I thought once more of the feel of the wet grass when I walked barefoot with dear Joanna at Hope in the sun-drenched dawn.

The riders were out, too, young couples, lone men, and several soldiers, one with a black manservant in brilliant livery trotting beside the horse.

"Quaco! Quaco! Papa, where is Quaco?" Johnny asked.

A sharp pain of remembrance pierced my heart. "He is no longer with me, Johnny," I replied. "By his own choice he has gone to live at the mansion of the Countess of Rosendaal. He went as a present from me to that great lady, and he will be there forever, I trust."

"Would you give me as a present also?" Johnny asked, a darkening cloud upon his face. "To that great lady or another?"

"No, never! You're mine now, my son. And together we will be, till life or death shall part us."

He looked at me and smiled. "Papa," he said. "Papa!"

My wife's pregnancy decreed that we move into lodgings in spite of the Macaulays' insistence that we were welcomed guests in their home. We took up lodgings with Mrs. Thompson, a self-styled xenophobe, bigot, and anti-abolitionist. She recognized my wife as Dutch and spurned her, although she respected me "as quality" and was civil to me. Johnny she pitied for having to call someone who could speak no English "Mama." We could not move, because Mrs. Thompson's house was clean, neat, and well appointed and the winter hard upon us. Besides, the roads to Devon, where we had chosen to live, were beset with cutthroats and highwaymen at that dark time of year.

I put Johnny to school at the Soho Academy with Mr. Baroes, a humane but strict headmaster. Johnny must have felt strange and burdened with sorrow at the loss of so doting a mother, yet he settled to learning and soon became popular with other scholars and also with the masters. Only once did he fight, in defense of his friend who was being bullied to misery. Johnny was a tall, strongly built lad.

At that time orphans were common in London, and Johnny asked me one day, "Am I an orphan or only partly one?"

"Not even partly," I replied. "In me you have your mother also and in Mama another mother. Three to take care of you, although only two seen."

"Mama cares not about me."

"How so?"

"By the way she carps at me and cossets herself. She frets that you do not beat me. She would like me frequently whipped."

"It is her disposition. She is easily made frantic."

"She spurns my mother as a slave."

"She does not! Think it not!"

He looked at me as Joanna would have done, but the words made me ponder. When Adriana and I had talked of Joanna before our marriage, it seemed like a fairy tale that began, "Once upon a time," and ended with the death of the beautiful princess. Now with Johnny present in our lives, the princess had been resurrected. How could I change the state of things? With my rapt attention Adriana grew more helpless, more hysterical. But then she was young, and with increasing age maturity would surely come upon her. She was a splendid woman, but all her instincts were those of a selfish child. There were constant quarrels with Mrs. Thompson in which, sadly, I became involved and on a point of principle sided with my dear.

Johnny and I walked all over London. He took me back to the happiest years of my life in spite of the tribulations of the Surinam jungle. He was the child of that time when my heart and soul were stirred by love's most tender sentiments and when as a roving youth I could distinguish love from the deadly sin of lust.

Johnny and I had gone walking in Hyde Park when my wife was confined. A fine, healthy boy was born to us as the frost lay hard upon the ground. We named him George William.

On the day of his baptism the weather turned so cold that icicles sprouted on my mustache, but Johnny was in his element. At the christening he placed his half-crown in George's fist and said, "Remember, George, this is the first money you have ever had in your life." This act endeared him to the assemblage and gladdened my heart.

I noticed that Adriana never smiled at Johnny. Her voice took on a stern flavor when she spoke to him. I questioned her about this.

"He is an obstacle in our life," she said in Dutch.

"I need him," I replied. "My need of him is in his presence—within him, his form, his face. He reminds me of people and places I once truly loved. Will you try not to remind me so often of what I truly detested in your people?"

When Johnny talked of Surinam I could detect that Joanna had told him in song, dance, story, and ritual of our great love. She had shown him the places where we had walked and sat in rapture, and Cery, his grand-mother, had conveyed him by barge to L'Esperance, now overrun by nature to take leave of the spot where our house had been and where the ghosts of our happiness awaited our return. We had always kept the anniversary of Joanna's death—he by pouring a libation of milk over the ground and me by praying for the peaceful rest of her soul.

As soon as the weather changed, Johnny and I attended the Theatre Drury Lane to see *School for Scandal*. Later in the spring we visited the Chelsea Academy to witness Dr. Blanchard, who invented the parachute, ascending into the heavens by the help of his balloon. Every tree and rooftop was awash with spectators. On the way back we met two Chinese men and I exhorted Johnny to embrace rather than fear their difference.

As soon as Adriana felt able to travel, we made preparations to leave London. To our surprise, Johnny announced that he had accidentally swallowed a pin an inch and a half long.

Adriana flew into a towering rage. "It will serve you right if it kills you," she raved. "Are you a lunatic?"

"Control your ire, my dear," I pleaded.

But she continued hysterical.

There was no reaction for five days. On the sixth day, however, he began to complain. By midnight he was desperately ill, and I set out at that hour to find a surgeon to bleed and physick the pin out of him. Adriana, who seemed unduly frantic at having sickness in the house, continued to argue his stupidity, which she somehow attributed to a taint of blood. I remonstrated with her and argued her stupidity as being located in her nationality, at which she became hysterical. The wet nurse for George at that moment arrived, and I was free to comfort my boy.

I was now a retired major on half-pension, but by the spring I had succeeded in leasing Henseley House, named after Robert Hensleigh, who owned lands at Tiverton, Devon, during the reign of Henry VIII. The house, a good brick building, was pleasantly situated, with convenient offices for a genteel family. After many tribulations we settled in and found our neighbors, the Dennys, friendly.

Johnny was in his element enjoying the lanes and fields with the Dennys' son, Tom, a playfellow of his own age. George grew more each day, but my wife found it hard to adjust to the customs of England. She quarreled with our servants, which was not the way of the English. Consequently there was a steady stream of servants leaving the parlor, the garden, and the kitchen.

When poor little George came down with the chicken pox, Adriana was beside herself, and she grew more distressed and angry when Johnny became sick, too. He developed no spots but had a fever. Adriana turned on Johnny, as we had no servants and he had been helping her while she lay in bed. That night he lay weeping in bed and I angrily asked her why she was so against him and why she never showed him any approval or regard, except when he was in service to her.

"I alone will nurse my boy," I said, "as his beauteous mother nursed me through the darkest hour of my tribulations and pain. Set your heart at ease. You will do nothing for him. You act as if the milk of human kindness is unknown to you."

My Johnny mercifully recovered. I fed him well and little George, too, since they were both pledged to the navy. George imitated Johnny, who was an enterprising lively chap, popular in the neighborhood and in the church, which he attended each Sunday. He never missed christenings, harvest suppers, and other social gatherings, was frequently invited to dine, and won the admiration of several ladies who greatly petted him. He was a generous, courageous, and obliging boy with a ready smile.

Adriana had developed very bad teeth, which started with her pregnancy. Dr. Smith decided that she should have one drawn, and she was extremely fearful. She begged Johnny to have one drawn also, and he consented to do so to help her through her fear. He missed school for some days. His usher, or assistant headmaster, called to acquaint him of the prize he had won for writing and, in his presence, give him a good character to us. He had been but a year at the school, and we drank his health.

Two days after the usher's visit, Adriana snapped at him, "A year at school. Tell me, what have you learned?"

"So much in one as you would in two," he replied, affronted.

Thereupon out shot her fist to give him a black eye. I was aghast. Was this not barbarity of another kind? I railed against the harshness of her blood and spoke of her inbred brutality, and after many high words between us she dissolved into her hysterics. This time it did not pass muster. But I pleaded with Johnny to ask her pardon to restore my peace of mind. I could cut his anger like a cake, but he obliged. She who had wronged him would not accept his apology, which further aggravated the situation. I spurned the dinner table, and so did she. Johnny had gone to school crying and returned with a letter of concern from the usher. I told her of the horror of her cruelty that she offered to the neighbors' view and to the community and suggested that, being Dutch, she would be slighted. When she walked abroad people whispered, "There goes Dutch Mrs. Stedman who gave her stepson a black eye for hatred's sake." And it was not the entire story. There was often peace and amity in my home.

When the mark was gone I drew a picture of my boy to show him that the damage had only been slight. The year was coming to a close; many good things had happened to me, even though I had wept at the loss of my beautiful peacock and my bees and hives. My wife, though hysterical, had seen Britain and learned English.

My wonderful boy had got his education. Young George and Sophie, my daughter recently born, were growing well, and I had learned experience. All my family were with me. We burned the "Ashen Log" at Christmas and were so hearty Johnny turned his glass once too often and was very drunk. I put him to bed at six o'clock on Christmas Eve. There was much laid in for the winter and all was well and God had shown us much mercy.

The children next door were being inoculated against the smallpox, which was not unknown in some parts of the country. I contacted Dr. Smith and he agreed to inoculate myself, George, and Johnny in the New Year.

Dr. Smith arrived promptly to do his job. After the inoculation I had no reaction, George had a few spots, but Johnny was extremely ill, since his pure Surinam blood had no resistance to disease. He was indeed very sick. As usual, Johnny's sickness triggered off Adriana's passion. She refused even to visit him. I sat at his bedside watching him toss and turn. Dr. Smith returned and said the disease must take its course.

"What shall I do?" Johnny gasped. "For you, to please you? Kill me! Kill me!"

"I won't leave you till you're better." I wept. "I won't leave you."

All night I watched him. Every minute I prayed alone by his bedside.

The next day he slept well. The crisis had passed. "How happy are you, Johnny, to awaken from this sleep, since numbers never do, they sleep the sounder first," I said.

"God will forever bless you, Papa," he replied.

"*Gado sa bressy* you." I smiled.

"*Gado sa bressy* you," he replied. "I saw my mama when I slept."

George came into the room. I watched him put his arm around his brother and kiss him. Soon after this we gave up Henseley House and moved to Broad Lane—a much finer residence.

Some inner purpose compelled me to seal up Johnny's papers. I put together his manumission certificate, the baptismal certificate, the deed changing his name from Robert to John, three papers from the colony of Surinam saying that he should never bear arms against the country of Surinam or prosecute the owners of Plantation Fauconberg for his enslavement but leave a quarter of his wealth to them should he die intestate and rich. I added a letter such as a father would offer to an eldest son.

That day when he returned from school I read my letter to him, for he would not see it again in my lifetime. He wept bitterly and in spite of all my comforting retired to bed with a heavy heart.

"What will become of me, Papa, if you die?" he sobbed.

"There is God, my son. He will take care of you."

The next day there appeared a confounding recklessness in him. He entered Mr. Moore's garden and took apples. He knew full well that we were in disagreement over a piece of land. Mr. Moore said much that should not have been said and threatened him with death. I leathered him for the first time in his life. He was twelve years old.

Out of his pocket fell a love token which he said had been given him by Betty Hobson, a sweet, shy young girl whose family lived a little way outside the town. We had met up once after church, and I recalled the glances they had exchanged. Miss Hobson was about eleven years old and knew that he was awaiting his call to the British he had put himself to school and to hairdressing and also to catechism, all in four months, although his hand was bad after he had fallen off a horse. I took him to the hangman, who, for a substantial fee, fixed it.

When it was healed, I discussed with Mr. Paul, the army schoolmaster, my desire that he supervise Quaco's education. But the man, violently disliking slaves, whom he called "Ham's children," insulted Quaco so damnably that Quaco wept and resisted, using insulting African language. It was called Coromantin, some words of which Mr. Paul understood. He was so shocked he disclosed his wishes in a letter to me to ban poor Quaco, now a fine lad, from school unless I whipped him soundly. I did not whip Quaco. I simply kept him home from the school.

Mr. Paul was outraged. "Blacks can only be checked by whippings," he insisted.

I offered him a drink, which he declined, so Quaco drank it down, much to Mr. Paul's annoyance. He left as the carrier brought me a letter from Mrs. Godefrooy, which I read before taking leave of him. It was a slight he fully deserved.

Dear John,

I thought of you on my birthday, which you have missed for the four years since you left Surinam. Although everyone else was here, the event was strangely muted. We danced, of course, and missed your delightful violin and singing. Joanna looked so beautiful in a yellow dress she had made. It is at such times when the mere mention of your name brings her to tears—I wish she would love again, but no other man is like you. Johnny is such a dear boy—a gentleman so early. God bless you, Stedman. Do come to us. I thank you for the money and navy. That week George caught the chicken pox and I prayed that the infant Sophie would not catch the sickness also. She did not, but because George was so attached to Johnny, he caught the sickness. It began with a harsh, hacking cough. We could not sleep for it. As usual, Adriana blamed the poor lad, ordering him like a beggar to a cold garret. Recalling the horrors of Surinam, I went mad and said that she was hateful and evil in the Dutch tradition. I put Johnny with Mrs. Rowes, a kindly woman who lived next door. After many alarms and altercations, Adriana insisted on having him back—a request which I peremptorily refused. I exhorted her to live with that devilry on her conscience. I spent much time with my boy—many gentle days—and had the satisfaction of seeing him get better. He was so ready to please her, and yet she found him untenable. Mrs. Rowes loved him as her own, and he often sought respite in her home when he was being harried by my wife in my absence.

As lieutenant colonel, a title of honor, I set about arranging Johnny's future. His call to join the navy came soon after. While I prepared his things we read the Bible together from cover to cover. At last the day came. He journeyed to Southampton to join his ship—the *Amity Hall,* bound for Jamaica. Another lad from Tiverton was with him. When he had gone, Adriana's temper improved, but Johnny returned in the summer, bringing an invitation for me from the captain of the *Royal William.* I accepted and we dined and danced in the wardroom, from where we got a fine view of the Isle of Wight. I spent a charming evening. The next day the army and the navy went into mourning for the Duke of Cumberland and Johnny appeared for the first time in full midshipman's uniform. He brought tears to my eyes. If only his dear mother could have seen our fine son now! I returned to Tiverton a happy man.

A year later Johnny arrived home. It was, in fact, the February of 1791. He carried a letter from his captain giving him a fine character and brought a present of a well-worked ship in a bottle for Mrs. Dennys. There was confidence and self-assurance about him, and he was most gracious when one of my friends presented him with a fine dress sword. He talked well and encouraged me to pursue my intention to publish my works. He had grown into a fine specimen of a man. But when his box arrived, it was almost empty. Everything was either lost or stolen or given away—even the hammock I had made for him.

I gave him such a sermon, which ended with him begging my pardon on his knees. For the rest of the time he was out with friends and, I suspect, whispering sweet nothings to Miss Hobson. He stayed at Tiverton, offering me much company, until the spring. We rode, sang, and played the violin. We walked and talked about life until on St. Patrick's Day he set off for Portsmouth with me to join the frigate *Lizard* as midshipman. I heard him telling Miss Hobson when he took leave of her at Halberton that he would go to the East Indies if God should order his return. I showed Miss Hobson the poem I had written on Joanna, and it brought bright tears to her eyes. She and Johnny were young and so much in love. I was sure she understood how firm my love had been.

Time passed slowly. Sometimes I rode with Adriana, as George was now at boarding school and another child, Robert, had been born to us. I was at this time able to write to Mr. William Blake, the engraver of my drawings, twice, thanking him for his efforts on my behalf. He never replied, but I did receive news of poor Quaco, who had been set adrift by Rosendaal. I was frantic and wrote a letter reminding her of her whoredoms in Steenbergen, where I was quartered, before she married the old man who did naught for her but as an act of redemption. She never replied. I then wrote to poor Quaco, alone in the world, asking him to come to me, and then to Adriana's brother to inquire of him. I learnt that he had returned from Holland to the warmth of Surinam and my heart eased, for I knew he would be happy there so many years after he had won his freedom.

The year had gone full-circle, and the summer had once again come. I anticipated my son's homecoming with an uplifted heart, but the days passed in disappointment. I began to fear the worst. None of the relations of the sailors on the *Lizard* had any news. And then I received a letter from the Admiralty. From the cold look of it my heart sank. The color left my cheeks, and with trembling hands I opened it. I was shot through with fire. The *Lizard* was lost in a storm off the coast of Jamaica with all hands. Sobs wracked my body and I lay shocked and wretched for days. Gone Joanna and now my boy! I could not restrain my tears. As the news spread, the house was overrun with mourners. The bell tolled in the church for my sweet boy's passing. George came home and could not be consoled, but for Adriana the sea had freed her from her fears and jealousies. Soon, however, she accused me of some intimacy with poor Betty Norman, a married lady wife of William Norman. My anger forced an apology in a letter to me.

Johnny was gone never more to return. Yet there were memories and none could interrupt me when and where I chose to turn those pages. My life flowed with the years, but to the end of my days the cloak of sorrow I wore for the loss of one so dear to me, though invisible to others, hung heavily about me. I could no longer be at peace in Tiverton and traveled extensively. From the way my life has turned I am consoled. God did not call my son away because I loved too much. I could not bear to think of him as dead. He and his friend had both looked so alive when last I saw them in Tiverton. Oh, the uncertainty of life! Yet Johnny's end was as it was destined to be. He is now with those who loved him well, his mother and Elizabeth Godefrooy, gone these long years. And together we will all be in spirit. He was but nineteen years old.

"Behold I have graven thee upon the palms of my hands; thy walls are continually before me." From these words I take my consolation and my strength. My Johnny! My sailor! My heart bleeds with sorrow at his dying, yet there can be no questioning of the will of God.